GOODBIRD
THE INDIAN

Goodbird and his son Donald, 1916.

GOODBIRD
THE INDIAN
HIS STORY

EDWARD GOODBIRD
as told to Gilbert L. Wilson

Illustrated by Frederick N. Wilson
With a new introduction
by Mary Jane Schneider

MINNESOTA HISTORICAL SOCIETY PRESS
St. Paul • 1985

♾ The paper used in this publication meets the minimum requirements of the American National Standard for Information Sciences — Permanence for Printed Library Materials, ANSI Z39.48-1984.

MINNESOTA HISTORICAL SOCIETY PRESS, ST. PAUL 55101

The frontispiece and the photograph on page xii are from the collections of the Minnesota Historical Society.

First published 1914 by Fleming H. Revell Company
New material copyright © 1985 by the Minnesota Historical Society
All rights reserved

International Standard Book Number 0-87351-188-3
Manufactured in the United States of America
10 9 8 7 6 5 4 3 2

LIBRARY OF CONGRESS CATALOGING-IN-PUBLICATION DATA

Goodbird, Edward
Goodbird the Indian.

Reprint. Originally published: New York : F. H. Revell Co., c1914.
Summary: A Hidatsa Indian man, living in North Dakota at the turn of the century, relates the story of his life and the history and customs of his people.
1. Goodbird, Edward. 2. Hidatsa Indians — Biography. 3. Hidatsa Indians — Social life and customs. 4. Indians of North America — North Dakota — Social life and customs. [1. Goodbird, Edward. 2. Hidatsa Indians — Biography. 3. Indians of North America — Biography] I. Wilson, Gilbert Livingstone, 1868-1930.

E99.H6G664 1985   978.4'00497 [92]   85-15583

Contents

Based on "Sketch Map of Fort Berthold Indian Reservation" traced by E. H. Coulson, 1930.

INTRODUCTION

The story of Edward Goodbird, Hidatsa Indian man from Fort Berthold, North Dakota, was originally written to teach Christian youngsters about other peoples and cultures, but it is more than a children's story. *Goodbird the Indian: His Story*, issued in 1914 by the Council of Women for Home Missions for their Interdenominational Home Mission Study Course, offers a rare, insider's view of historical events that were changing the lives of all Indian people. It is also a landmark in anthropological writing. Its author, Gilbert L. Wilson, anticipated other anthropologists by more than a decade in his use of biography to illuminate the culture he studied.[1]

Author's note: Part of the research on which this introduction is based was conducted while the author was a research associate at the Minnesota Historical Society on a project to develop an exhibition on Hidatsa cultural changes using the Gilbert L. Wilson collections. The generous financial and moral support of the staff of the Minnesota Historical Society is gratefully acknowledged. The author also wishes to thank the staffs of the State Historical Society of North Dakota and the Department of Anthropology at the American Museum of Natural History for their assistance in locating materials relating to Goodbird, Gilbert L. Wilson, and the Hidatsa.

[1] Although a few anthropologists had published personal documentaries, many consider the scholarly use of biographical literature to have begun with Paul Radin's *Crashing Thunder, the Autobiography of an American Indian* (New York: Appleton, 1926).

Perhaps because it was considered a children's book rather than a scholarly study of Hidatsa culture, the volume has been ignored, left unrecognized and out of print for most of its existence. Even Hidatsa scholars are unfamiliar with it. Gilbert Wilson suffered a similar lack of recognition during his lifetime, although his books were well received by the press and general public. His death in 1930 went unremarked in the anthropological community. In fact, it is easier to find obituaries of Goodbird than of Wilson.

Seventy years after the publication of *Goodbird the Indian*, we have an opportunity to bring both the book and its author out of obscurity. This new look incorporates a conception of the needs and future of Indian people and culture different from that accepted in the early years of this century. By using the documentary evidence in Wilson's papers, we can evaluate Wilson as biographer and Goodbird as subject. We can also add to this book the final pages of Goodbird's life.

Wilson's attitudes and actions were unusual for his time. *Goodbird* represents one of the few instances in which an anthropologist has sought to make ethnological information available to a popular audience and, even more remarkably, to children. Wilson was convinced of the need to produce good, accurate children's books about tribal cultures. He planned to write two more related biographies, collecting material for works on Goodbird's mother Waheenee (Buffalo Bird Woman, also known as Mahidiweash or Maxidiwiac) and her brother Wolf Chief, both children of Small Ankle. *Waheenee: An Indian Girl's Story* was published in 1921; the biography of Wolf Chief was never completed.[2]

In conceiving of his work as an educational trilogy for

children, Wilson also revealed his humanistic philosophy. Goodbird, Buffalo Bird Woman, and Wolf Chief were to him more than representatives of a strange way of life. In fact, the title *Goodbird the Indian: His Story* contrasts sharply with Wilson's personal approach to his subjects. (The title may have been selected by the editors for the Council of Women for Home Missions; in his foreword, Wilson refers to the volume as *Goodbird's Story*.) Nowhere in the narrative is Goodbird presented as "the Indian." He is always Goodbird, one man doing his best to cope with the upheaval of social and economic changes. Furthermore, although the title pages of both *Goodbird* and *Waheenee* indicate that their contents were written "as told to" Gilbert Wilson, in neither book is Wilson an active presence. That is the charm and strength of the books — there is a reality and immediacy to their subjects' lives. Because Goodbird and Buffalo Bird Woman were of different generations and genders, their stories offer an unusual opportunity to see tribal culture and the transition to reservation life through the eyes of two people with dissimilar personalities and experiences.

Wilson, too, must be understood as a player in the

[2] Maxidiwiac, as told to Gilbert Wilson, *Waheenee: An Indian Girl's Story* (St. Paul: Webb Publishing Co., 1921; Bismarck: State Historical Society of North Dakota, 1981; Lincoln: University of Nebraska Press, 1981). Details of Wolf Chief's story are in Alfred Bowers, *Hidatsa Social and Ceremonial Organization*, Bureau of American Ethnology Bulletin no. 194 (Washington, D.C.: Smithsonian Institution, 1965); Robert H. Lowie, "Societies of the Hidatsa and Mandan Indians," in *Anthropological Papers of the American Museum of Natural History* 11 (1916): 219–358; Gilbert L. Wilson, "The Horse and the Dog in Hidatsa Culture," in *Anthropological Papers of the American Museum of Natural History* 15 (1924): 125–311, and "Hidatsa Eagle Trapping," in *Anthropological Papers of the American Museum of Natural History* 30 (1928): 99–245.

drama of these lives. Born in Springfield, Ohio, in 1869, Gilbert Livingstone Wilson was the eldest of three children. Fascinated with Indians as a child, he studied Indian artifacts and history by reading as much as he could, and this contributed to his later interest in writing children's books on Indian mythology and culture. After graduating from Wittenberg College in Springfield, and obtaining a graduate degree in theology from Princeton Theological Seminary in 1899, he was ordained a Presbyterian minister and accepted pastorates, first in Minnesota and then in North Dakota. While serving as pastor of the Presbyterian church in Mandan, North Dakota, Wilson began to visit old Mandan and Hidatsa Indian village sites along the Missouri River and to attend Indian celebrations in the area. In 1905 he made a visit to Standing Rock Reservation, where he interviewed several Sioux people about their history and transcribed their stories. The same year he recorded a description of the speeches and discussion at a council of the Sioux chiefs with representatives from Washington, D.C.[3]

At some point, Wilson decided to publish the material he was gathering. Together with his brother Frederick, a talented artist, he began to plan several works on Indian mythology. Because Gilbert insisted that the illustrations be accurate, the two made a visit in 1906 to Fort Berthold Reservation, where Gilbert hoped to get answers to some of his questions about Indian artifacts, and Frederick

[3] For biographical information on Wilson, here and below, see Scrapbook, 1894–1928, in Gilbert Livingstone Wilson papers, Division of Archives and Manuscripts, Minnesota Historical Society (MHS). This collection also contains Wilson's reports and field notes for his trips from 1905 to 1908. The volume for 1905 and a separate notebook contain the record of his trip to Standing Rock and his description of the council meeting.

planned to make sketches that could be used as illustrations in later books.[4] Gilbert probably already knew Charles L. Hall, the Congregational missionary at Fort Berthold, since the religious community in western North Dakota was quite small in those days. At any rate, the brothers went first to Elbowoods, where they asked Hall for help on their project. Hall directed them to Independence, a farming community on the reservation; there they met Jessie McKenzie, a Congregational church worker, who introduced them to Wolf Chief and Goodbird. This meeting was the beginning of a collaboration between Gilbert Wilson and Goodbird's family that resulted in some of the finest information on Hidatsa culture that is available today.

By 1909 Wilson had been adopted into the Prairie Chicken clan and given the name Yellow-haired Prairie Chicken. This relationship had a profound effect on his work with the tribe. Hidatsa kinship was based on a system of family and clan membership that dictated behaviors and expectations.[5] Since clan membership passed through the mother, Goodbird, Buffalo Bird Woman, and Wolf Chief were all members of the Prairie Chicken clan. All the members of one's clan were treated as mothers, fathers, sisters, and brothers. Thus, through adoption, Wilson acquired a large family that was obligated to help him. Goodbird's father, Son-of-a-Star, was a member of a different clan, and his kinfolk — considered

[4] For examples of the brothers' children's books, see Gilbert L. Wilson, *Myths of the Red Children* (Boston: Ginn and Co., 1907) and *Indian Hero Tales* (New York: American Book Co., 1916).

[5] For a detailed study of Hidatsa kinship, see Bowers, *Hidatsa Social and Ceremonial Organization*. Goodbird's father Son-of-a-Star should not be confused with the better-known Arikara chief of the same name.

Wolf Chief and Gilbert L. Wilson
eating beef ribs, 1916.

to be aunts, uncles, and cousins — were also expected to
help out in time of need.

The relationship between Wilson and Goodbird was
rare even though adoptions of non-Indians were more
frequent in those years than they are today. Most anthropologists tried to maintain an objective stance by not
becoming overly involved with individuals. Wilson was
convinced, however, that the depth of information he
obtained was directly due to his adoption into the Prairie
Chicken clan. His letters and reports frequently refer to
these ties, and most of his acquaintances on the reservation were relatives of Goodbird. As a member of the family, Wilson was permitted to participate in reservation

events; Goodbird employed family connections in order
to help Wilson when Wilson began collecting objects for
the American Museum of Natural History. Wilson valued
the association. His training as a Presbyterian minister
and his later doctorate in anthropology never interfered
with his strong family feeling for his clan relatives.

Clan membership could, however, bring interesting
complications to the adoptee. In 1909 when Wilson married Ada Myers of Springfield, Ohio, he learned that his
bride, who had accompanied him to Fort Berthold Reservation, could not go with him to interviews. She was not
a member of the Prairie Chicken clan, and she could not
be adopted into the clan, since clan members were not
permitted to intermarry. In the Hidatsa way, Mrs. Wilson was an in-law and would be treated with respect, but
distantly, in the same way that any other in-law was
treated.[6]

Wilson sought to support his work on the Hidatsa by
collecting objects and information for museums. In 1907
he sold a small collection to George Heye, founder of the
Museum of the American Indian, Heye Foundation, in
New York City. Part of this collection was the sacred bundle of the Waterbuster clan, which Wilson bought from
Wolf Chief along with a complete account of its origin
and use. Wilson's first professional publication, a col-
laborative effort with George Pepper about the bundle,
appeared as a memoir of the *American Anthropologist* in
1908. The sale of the bundle caused a controversy that did
not die until the bundle was returned to the clan in 1938.
Tribal members questioned Wolf Chief's right to sell the

[6] Wilson to Clark Wissler, Curator of Natural History, November
6, 1909, Wilson correspondence file, 1909–77, American Museum of
Natural History.

bundle, and the curator of the State Historical Society of North Dakota believed that the bundle should have stayed in the state. But Wilson's adopted family stood by him, and his work continued despite the attempts of others to curtail it.[7]

In 1908, Wilson began to work for the American Museum of Natural History in New York, collecting a large number of Hidatsa articles and recording how they were made and used. Wilson, like other anthropologists of his time, wanted to preserve information about tribal life, particularly as it was lived before white traders, missionaries, and bureaucrats changed it. Unlike other anthropologists, however, he did not ask leading questions or offer interpretation. Instead, he wrote down what people told him. Comparisons of his handwritten journals with his typewritten reports to the American Museum of Natural History show that he usually introduced a topic, often agreed upon in advance with his informant, and then allowed the person to talk. Goodbird translated the Hidatsa into halting, but adequate, English, which Wilson wrote down. Later, Wilson used the English transcription to write his reports, in which he organized and corrected the original statements. Wilson always identified his own intrusion into the original speaker's thoughts, whether with a question or comment, and he distinguished his personal observations from what he was told. He dated all the entries and identified the speakers. His surviving field jour-

[7] Wilson and Pepper, "An Hidatsa Shrine and the Beliefs Respecting It," in *Memoirs of the American Anthropological Association* 2 (1908): 275–378; letter from O. G. Libby to Clark Wissler, September 5, 1908, O. G. Libby collection, State Historical Society of North Dakota (SHSND); Roy W. Meyer, *The Village Indians of the Upper Missouri* (Lincoln: University of Nebraska Press, 1977), 206–7.

nals show clearly the minimal nature of his editing and organizing; his reports are models of clarity and detail. Finally, Wilson edited the recorded material for publication by further organizing and rephrasing.[8]

Wilson's field notes and typed reports are considerably longer and more detailed than his published books and articles, and they are an important primary source of information on life on the reservation in the early days of this century. For example, Wilson was really interested only in the stories of life at Like-a-Fishhook Village, the home of the Mandan, Hidatsa, and Arikara (or "Ree") from about 1845 to the 1880s, but he also recorded Wolf Chief's lengthy autobiographical reminiscences that included details of reservation life at Independence. Today we recognize the latter information as a priceless aid to understanding how Indian men coped with the pressures of change and adapted to life as farmers and ranchers.

Goodbird the Indian is one of the products of Wilson's collecting and editing. Because of Goodbird's association with the Congregational church and his dealings with the federal government, he is also well represented in the documentary and photographic records of the church and the Bureau of Indian Affairs. Thus we have a rare opportunity to check this published biography with both the official records and Wilson's transcription of Goodbird's narrative.

Such a comparison allows us to add details and to evaluate Wilson's abilities as editor and anthropologist, ascertaining whether Wilson gave us an accurate portrait

[8] Wilson's field notes and copies of his reports to the American Museum of Natural History are in the Wilson papers, MHS. Goodbird's narrative autobiography is in "Report for 1913," p. 1–160.

of Goodbird or put words and ideas into his mouth. Obviously, some editing was necessary — Goodbird did not tell his story chronologically, and Wilson had limited space and a particular audience to consider. Not all the editorial changes, however, can be attributed to Wilson. In a letter to Robert H. Lowie, an anthropologist at the American Museum of Natural History, Wilson commented that the women who had edited the manuscript for use by the Interdenominational Home Mission Study Course had forced him to omit details of the self-sacrifices made during vision quests, judging them too cruel to be presented to children.[9] Wilson was angered by the decision, because he felt it was contrary to his goal of presenting a true picture of Indian life.

In the analysis of *Goodbird the Indian* that follows, the extent and nature of alterations made by Wilson and his editors becomes clear. In this discussion of the texts, "the narrative" refers to Wilson's transcription of his interview with Goodbird; "Wilson's version" is the book itself. Additional information has been provided to put the story in context.

When Goodbird was born, the Hidatsa were still living in Like-a-Fishhook Village, but many changes had

[9] Wilson to Lowie, May 28, 1914, Lowie correspondence, American Museum of Natural History. An interesting review of *Goodbird* in *The Word Carrier* (Santee, Nebr.), January–February 1915, p. 1, makes the same point, arguing that "There is already too much idealized Indian literature afloat. It raises no money and sends no missionaries. The women . . . should be ashamed of their folly." Since neither Wilson nor the reviewer mentions any other changes made by the Council, I have assumed that he is responsible for the additions to the text that are discussed below. Copies of *The Word Carrier* are available at MHS.

already taken place. The military had established a garrison nearby, traders had been living among the villagers for almost a century, and annuities and rations were distributed by the government's Indian agency in the village. Stone and bone tools had long since been replaced by metal, although bows and arrows were still preferred for hunting because bullets were scarce. Goodbird described the technological and social changes that surrounded him in his youth, rather than discussing precontact culture. Because he accepted the presence of the agents and military as part of his life, Goodbird does not deal with them specifically. Wilson sometimes had to explain situations and people that Goodbird took for granted.

The account of Goodbird's birth, near the mouth of the Yellowstone River around 1870, while the tribe was on a buffalo hunt, is a retelling of Buffalo Bird Woman's recollection (pages 6–12); Wilson recorded the same story in two of his other publications.[10] Goodbird's first memories were of his grandfather's lodge, the people who inhabited it, and the details of family life. While some of these memories appear in *Goodbird the Indian*, Goodbird's narrative contains many more details, including a floor plan of the lodge. He discussed the bathing practices of men and women at length, but Wilson added the description of Goodbird's "fat grandmothers" washing their faces (page 16); to Goodbird's memory of how his mother washed his face, Wilson also added, "I liked it quite as little as any white boy."

The family was prominent in the village. Goodbird's grandfather, Small Ankle, was keeper of the important

[10] Wilson, *Waheenee*, 156–74; Wilson, "The Horse and the Dog," 269–70.

Waterbuster clan sacred bundle, and both Son-of-a-Star
and Buffalo Bird Woman had acquired the rights to
sacred ceremonies. Small Ankle and Son-of-a-Star had
won success in warfare, indicating their leadership ability
and religious strength, and Buffalo Bird Woman was
noted for her modesty and industry. The religious leadership of the family may be related to Goodbird's later
prominence as a Christian leader. Despite the change in
religious systems, Goodbird followed the model of his
father and grandfather in later life.

Boys' hunting practices, reduced by Wilson to a few
paragraphs, were a large part of Goodbird's narrative. By
accompanying his brother Full Heart (or Full House, in
the sense of generous), Goodbird learned the habits of
different kinds of birds, how to hunt them with bow and
arrow, and how to snare them. Successful hunters, in pre-
paration for the day when they would give the meat to the
women of the household, took the birds to their mothers
or grandmothers, who cooked them and shared them with
the family. In this way, a boy not only learned the tech-
nical skills of hunting, but also the appropriate behavior
that accompanied hunting. Only by being an expert
hunter could a man hope to support his family. Even after
the Hidatsa began to farm and ranch, hunting continued
to be an important means of support, as it is today.

The most extensive of Wilson's editing begins with the
story of the dog travois (page 19) and runs through Chapters 3 and 4 on religion. All the material is taken from
conversations with Goodbird and other Hidatsa, but it
was not part of Goodbird's original autobiography. For
example, Goodbird mentioned the story of riding on the
dog travois during a discussion with Wilson of travois use.
Buffalo Bird Woman's belief that the change from earth-

lodge to log cabin had affected the life-span of her people was common to many Indians who found the new-style houses to be alien and lonely; she explained it to Wilson in her narrative. Some of Wilson's editorial comments on the treatment of children, like the final sentence of Chapter 2, are easily recognizable.

Nothing in the two chapters on religion badly misinterprets Hidatsa beliefs, and Wilson's interpolations stand out rather clearly, but it should be understood that the material was not part of Goodbird's autobiographical narrative. Goodbird told Wilson the anecdote of Minnie Enemy Heart (page 28) very early in their acquaintance to illustrate the problems of Christianity on the reservation. The version in *Goodbird the Indian* illustrates the accommodations made to bring Indian and non-Indian beliefs together. In the complete story, however, the vision ends with an argument that since white men, not Indians, crucified Jesus, Indians are Jesus' chosen people. Later conversations with Goodbird suggested that, in contrast to the statement on page 22, the Hidatsa did distinguish normal, everyday dreams from those that gave supernatural or spiritual power.

Wilson collected other information in these chapters at different times from different people, especially from Wolf Chief. The account of Wolf Chief's search for a vision was part of his autobiographical narrative, not Goodbird's. It is likely that the first intrusion of the Council of Women for Home Missions occurs here. We are not told that Wolf Chief was fastened to the post by thongs tied to skewers through his chest, and this omission makes the presence of wounds (page 25) inexplicable. Wolf Chief actually sought visions a number of times and never received any that his father thought were particularly significant; Wolf Chief set out to demonstrate that his visions were real by going on war parties. The treatment of Indian beliefs in Chapter 4 is based extensively on material supplied by Wolf Chief during the transfer of the sacred bundle of the Waterbuster clan to Wilson.

On the other hand, Goodbird's description of his school days is very close to that found in his narrative, although Wilson rearranged the material to fit a chronological pattern. In the description of the Christmas celebration (page 39–40) Wilson also added some explanatory material about the Christmas tree, an editorial comment that Goodbird and Hollis "acted as badly as two white children," and the statement, "I did not feel happy when I thought of this; but I was an Indian boy, and I was not going to forgive her for not giving me the magnet" (page 39). It should not be surprising to learn that "I am afraid I was a bad little boy" (page 41) is also Wilson's editorial comment. Some of the information about the school, like the account of the Friday dinners (page 42), came to Wilson from his friends the Halls; it helps to set the scene for subsequent descriptions of the work of the missionary.

Goodbird's discussion of his schooling is an important contribution to Indian history. Although later school experiences have been recalled and described by many Indian people, we rarely find such information about the early schools. The fact that Goodbird's parents let him make his own decision about school attendance reflects a familiar custom. The Hidatsa and other Indian tribes traditionally believed that children, particularly boys, should be allowed great freedom to test themselves and their abilities in order to learn to make decisions based on experience. Goodbird's adoption of the name Edward is another example of the decisions made by youngsters.

"Hunting Buffaloes," Chapter 6, comes straight from Goodbird's narrative; Wilson deleted some information to make the account more coherent. It gives good examples of the kinds of insight Wilson was able to elicit from his informants. Goodbird's depictions of how people behaved, the technology they used, and the way in which the hunt was conducted are consistent with other descriptions of Indian buffalo hunts, but they are here told with charming details that only a young man watching from the sidelines would notice. This is Wilson's classic style of collaboration with an informant.

The narrative description also contains many details about butchering and preserving the meat, additional comments on keeping buffaloes as pets, and mention of Goodbird's first buffalo kill, a calf which he shot with his rifle. Although calves were not normally hunted, the family was pleased with his success and ate the meat and gave away the hide. Goodbird also gave Wilson information on children's quarrels and trailing, but these were afterthoughts and not part of the original description of the hunt. From the original, Wilson omitted Goodbird's description of his first abortive attempt to kill an antelope and his family's reaction. When Goodbird came back to camp empty-handed, he was teased by his clan aunt, who had intended to claim his kill in keeping with Hidatsa tradition. Wilson's additions to the chapter include the comment, "I was proud of this vest, and cared not a whit that I had no coat to wear over it" (page 49). This is an obvious editorial comment, since wearing a coat with a vest was not part of Indian culture and so the lack of a coat would not have been of concern to Goodbird. Another bit of editorializing is found in the description of Goodbird's horse running with the others toward the hunt (page 52).

Goodbird told Wilson that he was "somewhat scared," but Wilson has him say "I tugged at the reins and clung to the saddle, too scared to cry out." By the age of twelve an Indian boy would be a competent rider and might be somewhat frightened, but it is unlikely that he would be as terrified as Wilson portrays him.

The section on farming and life at Independence is probably this book's most important contribution, because it gives a personal glimpse into the way in which one man and his family coped with enormous changes in their lives. The presentation is unemotional, without bitterness or complaint. Wilson briefly mentions the situation, but much more could be said about the kinds of changes that were taking place and the way they were introduced to the reservation. There is no mention of the Treaty of Fort Laramie of 1851 that set aside vast acres of land for the use of the Hidatsa, Mandan, and Arikara, nor of the executive orders that gradually reduced the land base to less than a million acres. Nowhere is there a discussion of the Indian agent's control in deciding who would be employed, who would get rations and annuities, who could leave the reservation for visits, and who would be punished for infractions of the rules against traditional dancing, religion, and medicine.[11]

Perhaps the greatest changes were brought about by allotment, a system under which Indian families were assigned separate parcels of land and encouraged to farm them. Administrators in the Office of Indian Affairs advocated the idea in the Treaty of Fort Laramie of 1868 with

[11] Here and in the paragraph below, see Meyer, *Village Indians.* Meyer provides a survey of the history of the Three Tribes with special emphasis on government relations.

the Sioux, and the policy was officially established by Congress in the General Allotment Act of 1887 (known as the Dawes Act). It was a controversial step. People who favored allotment believed that it would give each family the best chance to survive federal cuts in rations and annuities; in addition, individual ownership would stop the government's continuing reduction of the land base through executive orders. Proponents also hoped to give Indians civil rights and legal protection by allowing them to become citizens as they became landowners. But opponents of the measure, aware that Indian people were not used to individual landownership, knew tribal members could lose the land through sale or improper management; furthermore, the 160-acre parcels of land were not sufficient for farming or ranching in the arid West. In addition, selling surplus lands to non-Indians not only broke up the reservation, but also made it impossible for Indians to obtain additional land. Today almost 60 percent of the land included in the Fort Berthold Indian Reservation is owned by non-Indians.

The agent at Like-a-Fishhook argued that taking individual allotments would help people to become more self-reliant and give them greater access to reservation resources. Until the late 1870s, however, it was not practical for families to consider moving from Like-a-Fishhook, because the Sioux and other tribes that had forced the people into the village for protection were still a threat. By the time these enemies had been removed to reservations, the buffalo were also disappearing, the timber around the village had been used up, the soil in the garden lands was exhausted, and the village was overcrowded, so people were willing to move away. Groups of related families decided on an area, often a location that was known to them from winter camps or hunting trips, and moved there to establish farmsteads. Independence Hill was well known to members of Small Ankle's family; they moved there in about 1885. In his autobiographical narrative Goodbird discusses the delay in receiving title to the allotments, the difficulties of moving in summer, and the good hunting available in the area. Goodbird does *not* say, however, that the move to Independence "was a step toward civilization" or that "it had one ill effect: it removed me from the good influences of the mission, so that for a time I fell back into Indian ways" (page 56). Goodbird's words to Wilson were: "The first effect of our coming to Independence was to send me back to old ways. We could not, of course, live on the small rations that were issued to us and we had no gardens at Independence the first year. It was necessary for us to hunt a good deal to get enough to eat."[12]

The published story of Goodbird's vision quest does not vary much from the original narrative, except that details of how Turtle-no-head and Goodbird were attached to the posts are deleted. Goodbird said that Turtle-no-head had "his breast pierced and thongs tied to skewers in the wounds and these [were] fastened by a lariat to a forked post." The expurgated version leaves the reader to decide how he was suspended. In the same fashion, the published account of Goodbird's vision quest does not mention how Son-of-a-Star and a man called Crow pierced Goodbird's breast with Juneberry wood skewers and set up the post from which he suspended himself. Also omitted is a lengthy description of Goodbird's second vision quest. In his original narrative, Goodbird noted that

[12] Wilson, "Report for 1913," p. 56, Wilson papers, MHS.

his father was disturbed by the prohibition on Indian religion, but that he said very little about it. It was not uncommon for a young man to need to go through the vision quest a number of times before acquiring a strong spiritual helper, so both Son-of-a-Star's lack of concern over Goodbird's failure and his anger at the government for preventing further seeking were natural reactions for a Hidatsa father.

Some of the material about Goodbird's life as a farmer is also omitted from the book. In Wilson's version the agent explains how to measure an acre (page 60), but in the narrative Goodbird says that he went to the head farmer, Louis Sehie, for instructions on measuring one acre and ten acres.[13] The narrative also explains how the Indians used a threshing machine purchased by the government for the use of reservation residents and drawn by three horses. Each family could use the machine for a few days, and then it was passed on to the next family. As assistant farmer, Goodbird was in charge of the machine for his section of the reservation. He was also given responsibility for issuing rations when a distribution facility was established at Independence in order to save the families the long journey to Elbowoods.

Little is known about Indian ranching in western North Dakota, and it is unfortunate that neither Goodbird nor Wilson gives us more details. In order to provide an economic base for the reservation, the government furnished the Indians with cattle, and the agent assigned a brand to each rancher, but the cattle remained govern-

[13] Sehie is identified in *Annual Report of the Commissioner of Indian Affairs for 1895* (Washington, D.C.: Government Printing Office, 1895), 547.

ment property. Except for fences around crops and gardens, the reservation was unfenced. Cattle roamed at will and were rounded up and branded in the fall. (This general pattern continues today, with part of the reservation remaining unfenced and cattle ranging freely.) The agents were always concerned that the cattle received proper protection and care and, indeed, then as well as now, winter storms took their toll. Because the land was not fenced, the reservation's boundaries were unclear; although white ranchers were not supposed to graze their cattle on the reservation without a permit from the agent, the cattle of Indians and non-Indians often strayed across the boundaries. Indians complained bitterly about white cattle owners using their land, while the whites felt that Indian cattle straying onto their land should be redeemed by a cash settlement.

In the wild and rugged area of western North Dakota, cattle thieves were also a problem for both Indian and non-Indian cattlemen, so the story of Goodbird and his men trailing the stolen cattle is a familiar part of the area's history. In his narrative, Goodbird describes two different cattle searches, the first unsuccessful and the second occurring as described in the book (pages 61–64). In Goodbird's original account the thief is identified as Frank Paul, but Wilson gives the name as Frank Powers, perhaps to avoid any legal complications. In the records of brands issued in North Dakota in 1902, the brand described by Goodbird as belonging to Frank Paul — PO over the ribs on the right side — is registered to a man named Frank Poe of Williston, North Dakota. Goodbird also described a second trip to Powers's (Paul's, Poe's) ranch — the third trip in all — to look for more missing cattle.

Goodbird's position as assistant farmer was abolished about 1904,[14] and he was free to work as an interpreter for Wilson. He continued to farm but was ready for new employment when the Congregational missionary approached him seeking assistance with the church at Independence. Although Goodbird took his time in deciding to become a Christian, he never expressed any regret for giving up his traditional religion. Goodbird grew up in a religious family; perhaps, as a deeply religious person, he believed that any religion was better than none. Faced with the dilemma of choosing between no faith, due to the prohibition on Indian religion, or Christianity, Goodbird chose law-abiding Christianity. Others of his acquaintance were jailed and had their hair cut for continuing to practice traditional religion.[15] Goodbird's decision was undoubtedly influenced by his cousin George Bassett (mentioned on page 43) and by his early exposure to Christian education. Although Goodbird acted as an interpreter for Charles Hall when he preached at Independence, he was not baptized until 1905. From that time on he began to act as a church leader, although Hall continued to hope that a "young man of character and education" would be found to serve the church at Independence.[16] The young man never appeared, and Goodbird's

[14] Although Goodbird says that his position was abolished in 1903 (page 73), his name appears in the *Annual Reports of the Department of the Interior for . . . 1904: Indian Affairs* (Washington, D.C.: Government Printing Office, 1905), 1:638; he is not listed in the *United States Official Register . . . 1905* (Washington, D.C.: Government Printing Office, 1905).

[15] Religious freedom for Native Americans was finally guaranteed by the Native American Religious Freedom Act, passed by the United States Congress in 1978.

[16] Charles L. Hall, "Fort Berthold Notes," *The Word Carrier*, March 1907, p. 7.

success with the Congregational church at Independence gradually eliminated the need for a replacement.

The first church at Independence was a simple log building with a dirt floor. As Wilson describes the events (pages 69–71), the congregation at Independence decided around 1909 to raise the money to build a more elaborate chapel. Goodbird's narrative recalls that when the new chapel was dedicated in 1910, Gilbert Wilson preached the sermon, Frederick Wilson played the organ, and Robert Lowie gave five dollars. The church built by Goodbird and his relatives still stood in 1985 on the windswept plain at Independence, although it had been remodeled and relocated when the damming of the Missouri River forced the people to move away from the river's edge.

Wilson concluded *Goodbird the Indian* with a comment about the reservation and the predicted end of Indian ways, a sentiment totally in keeping with his times. In retrospect, however, his prediction was erroneous. His focus on earlier Indian life prevented him from seeing how Indians were adapting to white culture and, at the same time, maintaining as much of tribal culture as possible under the circumstances. Fortunately, because of his dedication and scholarship, Wilson wrote down whatever he was told, whether it fit his needs or not, and so he left us an unparalleled record of adaptation and adjustment.

Thus the final incident described in this book, Goodbird's account of the Decoration Day celebration (page 72), indicates both an acceptance of white ways, as Wilson and government officials preferred to understand it, and a continuation of the traditional customs of praising warriors and remembering the dead. Although Wilson does not analyze the material in *Goodbird the Indian*, he does leave clues for the interested reader, who may learn that the custom of having clan relatives decorate the graves maintains the traditional manner of dealing with the dead: clan relatives were expected to prepare the body and take it to the cemetery. Wilson also neglects to inform the reader that following the service at the cemetery, the clan relatives were given gifts, a further continuation of traditional behavior. In fact, the authorities who had encouraged the Decoration Day activities were horrified to find out that the traditional Indian give-away had become part of what they thought was a good example of the acceptance of a non-Indian ceremony. Today the give-away is an important part of many celebrations and always accompanies the funerals of specially loved or respected people.

This comparative analysis of *Goodbird the Indian* and Goodbird's personal recollections as told to Wilson shows that Wilson made two kinds of editorial changes. He added information that would clarify Goodbird's statements for white readers, and he interjected comments that would encourage the readers to view Goodbird as a human being, rather than as an Indian or representative of some strange culture. The deletions made by the Council of Women for Home Missions were significant in that they tend to mystify the reader by leaving out essential details, but they do not seriously damage the fabric of Goodbird's story.

Wilson, who had served as a minister in Minneapolis and St. Paul since 1907, made his last visit to the reservation in 1918. We have no record of later correspondence between him and Goodbird, although it is likely that they maintained some contact. Wilson's declining health and increasing pastoral responsibilities prevented him from making any more visits of record to the reservation; he turned to editing his reports for submission to the American Museum of Natural History and for publication. Wilson's doctoral dissertation, published by the University of Minnesota in 1917, was a description of Hidatsa agriculture based on information given him by Buffalo Bird Woman. As noted above, *Waheenee: An Indian Girl's Story* was published in 1921. Wilson intensified his scholarly work in the 1920s, teaching anthropology at Macalester College in St. Paul. Before his death in 1930, he published two scholarly monographs, "The Horse and the Dog in Hidatsa Culture" and "Hidatsa Eagle Trapping," based on his fieldwork. A third monograph, "The Hidatsa Earthlodge," was published posthumously, and his field notes have been used by others to create additional publications in his name.[17]

Goodbird's later life was occupied with farming and ranching, his work with Wilson, and his work with the church. Goodbird was considered a successful rancher, because his herd grew, because he was able to support his parents and his large family, and because his ranching operations were large enough to require that he employ several other men to work on his farm. His first grandchild of many was born at about the time *Goodbird the Indian* was published. Known as a good man, Goodbird was always ready to help those in need, whether Indian

[17] Wilson, "The Hidatsa Earthlodge," arr. and ed. Bella Weitzner, in *Anthropological Papers of the American Museum of Natural History* 33 (1934): 341–420; Wilson, "Mandan and Hidatsa Pottery Making," arr. and ed. W. Raymond Wood and Donald J. Lehmer, in *Plains Anthropologist* 22 (1977): 97–106; Bella Weitzner, "Notes on the Hidatsa Indians Based on Data Recorded by the Late Gilbert L. Wilson," in *Anthropological Papers of the American Museum of Natural History* 56 (1980): 183–322. See also notes 1 and 2, above.

or non-Indian. He kept up the custom of sharing whatever he had, whether food or time, and so he was respected and loved throughout the community. He once complained to Wilson that he had stopped raising hogs because whenever he butchered one he gave so much meat away that the remainder fed his family for only four days.[18] Although Wilson and Goodbird became close associates, it is doubtful that Wilson's presence changed Goodbird's life. Goodbird simply added Wilson into the family as another person who needed his help.

Goodbird's work with the church increased steadily toward the end of his life. According to columns written by Charles L. Hall and others, in 1915 the Congregational church decided to license three of the Indian men who had been working closely with the three church stations on the reservation. Goodbird took the job and gave up his other work in order to spend full time in church work. In 1925 Goodbird was ordained in a joyous, all-day celebration that included representatives of six English-speaking and two Indian-speaking churches. In the morning Goodbird was questioned about his faith and Christian experience, and in the afternoon he was ordained to become the first Indian Congregational minister on the reservation. Wolf Chief, adding an interesting note of Hidatsa ceremony, then sponsored a feast in honor of his son Paul, who had died recently. Goodbird's work included preaching, visiting members of his congregation, attending annual convocations of the reservation's Congregational churches, and myriad other duties that befell a skilled interpreter. In order to get around to his people, Goodbird learned to drive a car as well as he once rode

[18] Wilson, "Report for 1913," p. 154, Wilson papers, MHS.

a horse or drove a wagon, and for ten years he was a common sight going about his work.[19]

In 1935 Goodbird began to suffer serious problems with his legs and had difficulty walking. In recognition of his years of service, the national office of the Congregational church awarded him an annuity; in 1936 he officially retired from his position as pastor of the Independence Congregational Church. Despite Goodbird's retirement and infirmity, H. W. Case, Hall's successor at the Congregational mission, noted that he continued to serve as pastor, and Case requested that the church's head office grant Goodbird about eight dollars a month for gasoline expenses.[20] In mid-August 1938, Goodbird attended the Annual Fellowship of Congregational Churches on the reservation and later went to a funeral service. Toward the end of the month, however, he suffered a stroke, and he died a few days later. He was buried in the church cemetery at Independence where stone monuments mark his grave and those of his relatives.[21]

Beneath Wilson's asides and the women's expunging of details of self-mutilation, *Goodbird the Indian* remains an inspiring story of an ordinary man caught up in the threads of cultural change. At his birth, his people were still using dogs to carry their goods from place to place. At his death, airplanes were replacing trains. How Goodbird adapted to these transformations, some forced by

[19] Newspaper clippings in Scrapbooks 1 and 3, Case collection, SHSND. On Goodbird's ordination, see Harold W. Case, *100 Years at Fort Berthold* (Bismarck, N.Dak.: Bismarck Tribune, 1976), 342–43.

[20] Case to Goodbird, December 20, 1935, Case to Rev. Fred L. Brownlee, November 17, 1936, in Case collection, SHSND.

[21] *McLean County Independent* (Garrison, N.Dak.), September 4, 1938, p. 1.

well-meaning government agents and others introduced simply by contact with non-Indians, is relevant not only to our understanding of American Indians, but also to ourselves in our world of accelerating change. People can and do adapt to tumultuous changes with grace and vigor, even joy, and we can all take heart from Goodbird's message.

Glossary of Indian Words

a̤ ha̤ hé̱

aī (ĭ)

a̤ pa̤ típ

E̱ dī á ka̤ ta̤

Hĭ dắt sa̤

Hō Wash té̱

Ĭt sĭ dī shĭ dī í ta̤ ka̤

Ĭt sĭ ka̤ mä́ hĭ dī

Ka̤ dū́ te̱ ta̤

kū kats

Ma hĭ́ dī wī a̤

Mắn dăn

mĭ há́ dīts

Mĭ nĭ tä́ rĭ

na̤

Săn té̄ē

Sioux (Sō̄ō). (The plural, spelled also Sioux, is commonly pronounced Soos.)

té̆ pē̄ē

Tsa̤ ká̤ ka̤ sa̤ kĭ

Tsá̤ wa̤

ū a̤ kĭ hĕ kĕ

FOREWORD

CATLIN in 1832, and Maximilian in 1833, have made famous the culture of the Mandan and Minitari, or Hidatsa, tribes.

In 1907, I was sent out by the American Museum of Natural History, to begin anthropological studies among the remnants of these peoples, on Fort Berthold Reservation; and I have been among them each summer, ever since.

During these years, Goodbird has been my faithful helper and interpreter. His mother, Mahidiwia, or Buffalo Bird Woman, is a marvelous source of information on old-time life and beliefs.

Indians have a gentle custom of adopting very dear friends by relationship terms; by such adoption, Goodbird is my brother; Mahidiwia is my mother.

The stories which make this little book were told me by Goodbird in August, 1913.

I have but put Goodbird's Indian-English into common idiom. The stories are his own; in them he has bared his heart.

In 1908, and again in 1913, my brother, Frederick N. Wilson, was also sent by the Museum to make drawings of Hidatsa arts. Illustrations in this book are from studies made by him in those years; a few are redrawn from simpler sketches by Goodbird himself.

FOREWORD

Acknowledgment is made of the courtesy of the Museum's curator, Dr. Clark Wissler, whose permission makes possible the publishing of this book.

May *Goodbird's Story* give the reader a kindly interest in his people.

Minneapolis.   G. L. W.

GOODBIRD THE INDIAN

An Old Hidatsa Village.

I

BIRTH

I WAS born on a sand bar, near the mouth of the Yellowstone, seven years before the battle in which Long Hair * was killed. My tribe had camped on the bar and were crossing the river in bull boats. As ice chunks were running on the Missouri current, it was probably the second week in November.

The Mandans and my own people, the Hidatsas, were once powerful tribes who dwelt in five villages at the mouth of the Knife River, in what is now North Dakota. Smallpox weakened both peoples; the survivors moved up the Missouri and built a village at

* General George A. Custer.

Like-a-fish-hook Bend, or Fort Berthold as the whites called it, where they dwelt together as one tribe. They fortified their village with a fence of upright logs against their enemies, the Sioux.

We Hidatsas looked upon the Sioux as wild men, because they lived by hunting and dwelt in tents. Our own life we thought civilized. Our lodges were houses of logs, with rounded roofs covered with earth; hence their name, earth lodges. Fields of corn, beans, squashes and sunflowers lay on either side of the village, in the bottom lands along the river; these were cultivated in old times with bone hoes.

With our crops of corn and beans, we had less fear of famine than the wilder tribes; but like them we

Bone Hoe.

hunted buffaloes for our meat. After firearms became common, big game grew less plentiful, and for several years before my birth, few buffaloes had been seen near our village. However, scouts brought in word that big herds were to be found farther up the river and on the Yellowstone, and our villagers, Mandans and Hidatsas, made ready for a hunt.

A chief, or leader, was always chosen for a tribal hunt, some one who was thought to have power with the gods. Not every one was willing to be leader. The tribe expected of him a prosperous hunt with plenty of meat, and no attacks from enemies. If the hunt proved an unlucky one, the failure was laid to the leader. " His prayers have no power with the gods. He is not fit to be leader! " the people would say.

This leader had to be chosen by a military society of men, called the Black Mouths. They made up a collection of rich gifts—gun, blankets, robes, war bonnet, embroidered shirt—and with much ceremony offered the gifts, successively, to men who were known to own sacred bundles; all refused.

They prevailed at length upon Ediakata to accept half the gifts. "Choose another to take the rest," he told the Black Mouths: "I will share the leadership with· him!" They chose Short Horn.

The two leaders fixed the day of departure. On the evening before, a crier went through the village, calling out, "To-morrow at sunrise we break camp. Get ready, everybody!"

The march was up the Missouri, on the narrow prairie between the foothills and the river. Ediakata and Short Horn led, commanding, the one, one day, the other, the next. The camp followed in a long line, some on horseback, more afoot; a few old people rode on travois. Camp was made at night in tepees, or skin-covered tents.

My grandfather's was a large thirteen-skin tepee, pitched with fifteen poles. It sheltered twelve persons; my grandfather, Small Ankle, and his two wives, Red Blossom and Strikes-many-woman; his sons, Bear's Tail and Wolf Chief, and their wives; my mother, Buffalo Bird Woman, daughter of Small Ankle, and Son-of-a-Star, her husband; Flies Low, a younger son of Small Ankle; and Red Kettle and Full Heart, mere boys, brothers of Flies Low.

Ascending the west bank of the Missouri, my tribe reached the mouth of the Yellowstone at their eleventh camp; here the Missouri narrows, offering a good place to cross. A long sand bar skirted the south shore; tents were pitched here about noon. There was not room on the narrow bar to pitch a camping circle, and the tepees stood in rows, like the houses of a village.

My grandfather pitched his tent near the place chosen for the crossing. The day was cold and windy; with flint and steel, my grandfather kindled a fire. Dry grass was laid around the wall of the tent and covered with robes, for beds. Small logs, laid along the edges of the beds, shielded them from sparks from the fire.

At evening the wind died; twilight crept over the sky, and the stars appeared. The new moon, narrow and bent like an Indian bow, shone white over the river, and the waves of the long mid-current sparkled silvery in the moonlight. Now and then with a *swi-i-s-sh*, a sheet of water, a tiny whirl-pool in its center, would come washing in to shore; while over all rose the roar, roar, roar of the great river, sweeping onward, the Indians knew not where.

At midnight a dog raised himself on his haunches, pointed his nose at the sky, and yelped. It was the signal for the midnight chorus; and in a moment every dog in camp had joined it, nose-in-air, howling mournfully at the moon. Far out on the prairie rose the wailing yip-yip-yip-*ya-a-ah!* of a coyote. The dogs grew silent again and curled up, to sleep.

And I came into the world.

Wrapped in a bit of robe, I was laid in my mother's arms, her first born; she folded me to her breast.

The morning sky was growing gray when my father came home. He raised the tent door and entered, smiling.

" I heard my little son cry, as I came," he said;
" It was a lusty cry! I am very happy."

My grandmother placed me in his arms.

My tribe began crossing the river the same morning.
Tents were struck, one by one; and the owners, having
loaded their baggage in bull boats, pushed boldly out
into the current.

A bull boat was made by stretching a buffalo skin
over a frame of willows. It was shaped like a tub and
was not graceful; but it carried a heavy load.

Our boat had been brought up from the village on a
travois, and my father ferried my mother and me
across. He knelt in the bow, dipping his oar in the
water directly before him; my mother sat in the tail
of the boat with me in her arms. Our tent poles,
tied in a bundle, floated behind us; and our dogs and
horses came swimming after, sniffing and blowing as
they breasted the heavy current. We landed tired,
and rather wet.

The tribe was four days in crossing; and as the
season was late, we at once took up our march to the
place chosen for our winter camp. My mother and I
now rode on a travois, drawn by a pony. A buffalo
skin was spread on the bottom of the travois basket;
this my father bound snugly about my mother's knees
as she sat, Indian fashion, with her ankles turned to
the right. I lay in her lap, cuddled in a wild-cat skin
and covered by her robe.

We reached Round Bank, the place of our winter
camp, in five days. My tribe's usual custom was to
winter in small earth lodges, in the woods by the Missouri, a few miles from Like-a-fish-hook village; but

this winter we were to camp in our skin tents, like
the Sioux. A tent, well sheltered, with a brisk fire
under the smoke hole, was comfortable and warm.

No buffaloes had been killed on the way up to the
Yellowstone; but much deer, elk, and antelope meat
had been brought into camp, dried, and packed in bags
for winter. Many, also, of the more provident families
had stores of corn, brought with them from Like-a-fish-
hook village. After snow fell, our hunters discovered
buffaloes and made a kill. We thus faced winter without fear of famine.

The tenth day after my birth was my naming day;
it came just as we were getting settled in our winter
camp. An Indian child was named to bring him good
luck. A medicine man was called in, feasted, and given
a present to name the child and pray for him. As my
grandfather was one of the chief medicine men of the
tribe, my mother asked him to name me.

My grandfather's gods were the birds that send the
thunder. He was a kind old man, and took me gently
into his arms and said, " I name my grandson *Tsa-
ka-ka-sa-ki*,—Good-bird!" My name thus became a
kind of prayer; whenever it was spoken it reminded
the bird spirits that I was named for them, and that
my grandfather prayed that I might grow up a brave
and good man.

The winter passed without mishap to any one in our
tent. An old man named Holding Eagle had his leg
broken digging in a bank for white clay; he was prying
out a lump with a stick, when the bank caved in upon
him. Toward spring, Wolf-with-his-back-to-the-wind
and his brother were surprised by Sioux and killed. A
man named Drum was also killed and scalped.

Spring came, but ice still lay on the Missouri when the Goose society gave their spring dance. The flocks of geese that came flying north at this season of the year were a sign that it was time to make ready our fields for planting corn. The Goose society was a society of women, and their dance was a prayer that the spirits of the geese would send good weather for the corn-planting. Most of the work of planting and hoeing our corn fell to the women.

Our winter camp now broke up, most of the tribe returning to the Yellowstone; but my grandfather and One Buffalo, with their families, went up the Missouri to hunt for buffaloes. They found a small herd, gave chase, and killed ten.

Four more tepees now joined us, those of Strikes Back-bone, Old Bear, Long Wing, Spotted Horn, and their families. To each tent owner, my grandfather gave the half of a freshly killed buffalo and one whole green buffalo skin. Camp was pitched; the meat was hung on stages to dry, and the women busied themselves making the skins into bull boats.

At Work with a Bone Hoe.

When the ice on the Missouri broke, our camp made ready to return to the village, for the women wanted to be about their spring planting. Bull boats were now taken to the river and loaded; and the families, six or seven tepees in all, pushed out into the current.

My parents led, with three boats lashed together, in the first of which they sat and paddled; my father's rifle lay by him. The second boat was partly loaded with bags of dried meat, and upon these sat Flies Low, my uncle, with me in his arms. The third boat was loaded to the water with meat and skins.

The Missouri's course is winding; if a turn in it sends the current against the wind, the waves rise heavy and choppy, so that a single boat can hardly ride them. When approaching one of these turns, our party would draw together, laying tight hold of one another's boats until the danger was passed; bunched together in this manner, the boats ran less risk of upsetting.

Snow had disappeared from the ground, and the grass was beginning to show green when we left the Yellow-stone. We floated down the great river in high spirits. All went well until we neared the mouth of the Little Missouri, thirty miles from the village. Then a storm arose, and as we rounded a bend, the current carried us into the very teeth of the wind. Our flimsy boats, sea-sawing up and down on the heavy waves, threatened to overturn.

My parents turned hastily to shore and plied their paddles. Suddenly my father leaned over his side of the boat, almost tipping it over and tumbling my mother in upon him; she caught at the edge of the boat to save herself, but had the presence of mind not to drop her paddle. Then she saw what had happened; I had fallen into the water, and my father was drawing me, wet but unhurt, into the boat.

I have said that my uncle, Flies Low, and I rode in

the second boat. I had grown restless, and he had loosened my cradle clothes to give me room to move my limbs. When we ran into the storm, our boat rocked so violently that I slipped from his arms, but my loosened clothes made me float.

" I did not mean to drop the baby," my uncle said afterwards. " I thought the boat had upset and I was frightened." He was only a lad, and my mother could not blame him.

We reached shore in a terrible storm of snow and wind. The boats were dragged up on the beach; the two tents were hastily pitched to shelter the women and children; and fires were lighted.

My father stopped only long enough to see us safe, and then pushed on through the storm with the horses, which my grandfather had been driving along the shore in sight of the boats. He reached the village safely and drove the horses into the shelter of some woods along the river.

Boys know that in summer, when they go swimming, it is warmer to stay in the water, than upon the bank, in a wind. There was a pond in the woods; and our horses waded into the water to escape the

Flint and Steel, with Bag.

cold wind. When they came out the wind chilled their coats, so that three of them died.

The storm lasted four days. When it was over, my

mother and the rest of the party re-embarked in their bull boats and floated safely down to Like-a-fish-hook village.

Of course I remember nothing of these things; but I have told the story as I heard it from the lips of my mother.

Hidatsa Earth Lodge.

II

CHILDHOOD

LIKE-A-FISH-HOOK village stood on a bluff overlooking the Missouri, and contained about seventy dwellings. Most of these were earth lodges, but a few were log cabins which traders had taught us to build.

My grandfather's was a large, well-built earth lodge, with a floor measuring about forty feet across. Small Ankle, his two wives and their younger children; his sons, Bear's Tail and Wolf Chief, and his daughter, my mother, with their families, dwelt together. It was usual for several families of relatives to dwell together in one lodge.

An earth lodge was built with a good deal of labor. The posts were cut in summer, and let lie in the woods until snow fell; men then dragged them to the village with ropes. Holes were dug the next spring, and the posts raised. Stringers, laid along the tops of the posts, supported rafters; and upon these was laid a matting of willows and dry grass. Over all went a thick layer of sods.

The four great posts that upheld the roof had each

a buffalo calf skin or a piece of bright-colored calico bound about it at the height of a man's head. These were offerings to the house spirit. We Hidatsas believed that an earth lodge was alive, and that the lodge's spirit, or soul, dwelt in the four posts. Certain medicine women were hired

Small Ankle's Couch.

to raise these posts in place when a lodge was built.

Our lodge was picturesque within, especially by the yellow light of the evening fire. In the center of the floor, under the smoke hole, was the fireplace ; a screen of puncheons, or split logs, set on end, stood between it and the door. On the right was the corral, where horses were stabled at night. In the back of the lodge were the covered beds of the household, and my grandfather's medicines, or sacred objects. The most important of these sacred objects were two human skulls of the Big Birds' ceremony, as it was called. Small Ankle was a medicine man and when our corn fields suffered from drought, he prayed to the skulls for rain.

Against the puncheon screen on the side next the fireplace, was a couch made of planks laid on small logs, with a bedding of robes. This couch was my grandfather's bed at night, and his lounging place by day. A buffalo skin overhead protected him from bits of falling earth or a leak in the roof, when it rained.

My two grandmothers also used the couch as a bench when making ready the family meals; and the water and grease spilled by them and trampled into the dirt floor made the spot between the couch and the fireplace as hard as brick. Small Ankle filed his finger nails here against the hard floor.

The earliest thing that I remember, is my grandfather sitting on his couch, plucking gray hairs from his head. Indians do not like to see themselves growing old, and Small Ankle's friends used to tease him. "We see our brother is growing gray—and old!" they would say, laughing. Small Ankle used to sit on the edge of his couch with his face tilted toward the smoke hole, and drawing his loose hair before his eyes, he would search for gray ones.

He had another habit I greatly admired. The grease dropped from my grandmothers' cooking, drew many flies into our lodge, and as my grandfather sat on his couch, the flies would alight on his bare shoulders and arms. He used to fight them off with a little wooden paddle. I can yet hear the little paddle's *spat* as it fell on some luckless fly, against his bare flesh. No war club had surer aim.

His couch, indeed, was the throne from which my grandfather ruled his household, and his rule began daily at an early hour. He arose with the birds, raked coals from the ashes and started a fire. Then we would hear his voice, " Awake, daughters; up, sons; out, all of you! The sun is up! Wash your faces! "

My fat grandmothers made a funny sight, washing their faces; stooping, with eyes tightly shut, each filled her mouth with water, blew it into her palms and rubbed them over her face. No towels were used.

The men of the household more often went down for a plunge in the river. Some of the young men of the village bathed in the river the whole year, through a hole in the ice in winter.

Many bathers, after their morning plunge, rubbed their wet bodies with white clay; this warmed and freshened the skin.

My mother usually washed my face for me; I liked it quite as little as any white boy.

Our morning meal was now eaten, hominy boiled with beans and buffalo fat, and seasoned with alkali salt—spring salt we called it, because we gathered it from the edges of springs. After the meal, I had nothing to do all day but play.

My best loved toy was my bow, of choke-cherry wood, given me when I was four years old. My arrows were of buck-brush shoots, unfeathered. These shoots were brought in green, and thrust into the hot ashes of the fireplace ; when heated, they were drawn out and the bark peeled off, leaving them a beautiful yellow. Buck-brush arrows are light, and I was allowed to shoot them within the lodge.

My uncle, Full Heart, a boy two years older than

myself, taught me how to use my bow. In our lodge were many mice that nested in holes under the sloping roof, and my uncle and I hunted these mice as savagely as our fathers hunted buffaloes. I think I was not a very good shot, for I do not remember ever killing one.

But I had the ill luck to shoot my mother. She was stooping at her work, one day, when an arrow badly aimed struck her in the cheek, its point pierced the skin, and the shaft remained hanging in the flesh. I saw the blood start and heard my mother cry, " Oh, my son has shot me! " I dropped my bow and ran, for I thought I had killed her; but she drew out the shaft, laughing.

I was too young to have any fear of the Sioux, and I had not yet learned to be afraid of ghosts, but I was afraid of owls, for I was taught that they punished little boys. Sometimes, if I was pettish, my uncles would cry, " The owl is coming! " And in the back of the lodge a voice would call, " *Hoo, hoo, hoo!* " This always gave me a good fright, and I would run to my grandfather and cover my head with his robe, or hide in my father's bed.

It was not the custom of my tribe for parents to punish their own children; usually, the father called in a clan brother to do this. My uncle, Flies Low, a clan brother of my father, punished me when I was bad, but he seldom did more than threaten.

Sometimes my mother would say, " My son is bad, pierce his flesh! " and my uncle would take an arrow, pinch the flesh of my arm, and make as if he would pierce it. I would cry, " I will be good, I will be good! " and he would let me go without doing more than giving me a good fright.

A very naughty boy was sometimes punished by rolling him in a snow bank, or ducking him in water.

One winter evening I was vexed at my mother and would not go to bed. " Come," she said, trying to draw me away, but I fought, kicking at her and screaming. Quite out of patience, my mother turned to Flies Low. " *Apatip*—duck him! " she cried. A pail of water stood by the fireplace. Flies Low caught me up, my legs over his shoulder, and plunged me, head downward, into the pail. I broke from him screaming, but he caught me and plunged me in again. The water strangled me, I thought I was going to die!

" Stop crying," said my uncle.

My mother took me by the arm. " Stop crying," she said. " If you are bad, I will call your uncle again! " And she put me to bed.

We Indian children knew nothing of marbles or skates. I had a swing, made of my mother's packing strap, and a top, cut from the tip of a buffalo's horn. Many boys owned sleds, made of five or six buffalo ribs bound side by side. With these they coasted down the steep Missouri bank, but that was play for older boys.

Sled of Buffalo Ribs.

Few wagons were owned by the tribe at this time. When journeying, we packed our baggage on the backs of ponies, or on travois dragged by dogs.

A travois was a curious vehicle. It was made of two poles lashed together in the shape of a V, and bearing a flat basket woven with thongs. A good dog with a travois could drag sixty or eighty pounds over the snow, or on the smooth prairie grass.

But a travois's chief use was in dragging in wood for a lodge fire. In our lodge my mother and my two grandmothers, with five dogs, went for wood about twice a week. They started at sunrise for the woods, a mile or two away, and returned about noon.

It happened one morning that my father and mother went to gather wood, and I asked to go along. " No," they said, " you would but be in our way. You stay

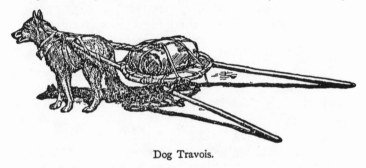

Dog Travois.

at home! " But I wept and teased until they let me go.

My parents walked before, the dogs following in a single file. They were gentle animals, used to having me play with them; and I was amusing myself running along, jumping on a travois, riding a bit, and jumping off again.

Our road led to a choke-cherry grove, but it was crossed by another that went to the river. As we neared the place where the roads crossed, we saw a woman coming down the river road, also followed by three or four dogs in travois. I had just leaped on the travois of one of our dogs.

The packs spied each other at the same instant; and

our dogs, pricking up their ears, burst into yelps and started for the other pack. I was frightened out of my wits. "*Ai, ai, ai!*" I yelled; for I thought I was going to be eaten up. The dogs were leaping along at such speed that I dared not jump off.

The woman with the strange dogs ran between the packs crying, "*Na, na,*—go way, go way!" This stopped our dogs; and I sprang to the ground and ran to my mother. I would never ride a travois again.

Taking it altogether, children were well treated in my tribe. Food was coarse, but nourishing; and there was usually plenty of it. Children of poor families suffered for clothing, but rarely for food, for a family having meat or corn always shared with any who were hungry. If a child's parents died, relatives or friends cared for him.

My mother sighs for the good old times. "Children were then in every lodge," she says, "and there were many old men in the tribe. Now that we live in cabins and eat white men's foods, the children and old men die; and our tribe dies!"

But this is hardly true of the Christian families.

III

THE GODS

I HAVE said we Hidatsas believed that an earth lodge was alive; and that its soul, or spirit, dwelt in the four big roof posts. We believed, indeed, that this world and everything in it was alive and had spirits; and our faith in these spirits and our worship of them made our religion.

My father explained this to me. "All things in this world," he said, " have souls, or spirits. The sky has a spirit; the clouds have spirits; the sun and moon have spirits; so have animals, trees, grass, water, stones, everything. These spirits are our gods; and we pray to them and give them offerings, that they may help us in our need."

We Indians did not believe in one Great Spirit, as white

Seeking His God.

21

men seem to think all Indians do. We did believe that certain gods were more powerful than others. Of these was *It-si-ka-ma-hi-di*, our elder creator, the spirit of the prairie wolf; and *Ka-du-te-ta*, or Old-woman-who-never-dies, who first taught my people to till their fields. Long histories are given of these gods.

Any one could pray to the spirits, receiving answer usually in a dream. Indeed, all dreams were thought to be from the spirits; and for this reason they were always heeded, especially those that came by fasting and suffering. Sometimes a man fasted and tortured himself until he fell into a kind of dream while yet awake; we called this a vision.

A man whom the gods helped and visited in dreams, was said to have mystery power; and one who had much mystery power, we called a mystery man, or medicine man. Almost every one received dreams from the spirits at some time; but a medicine man received them more often than others.

A man might have mystery power and not use it wisely. There once lived in our village a medicine man who had one little son. On day in summer, the little boy with some playmates crossed a shallow creek behind the village in search of grass for grass arrows. It happened that the villagers' fields were suffering from drought, and that very day, some old men brought gifts to the medicine man and asked him to send them rain.

The medicine man prayed to his gods, and in an hour rain fell in torrents. The little boys, seeking to return, found the creek choked by the rising waters; **greatly frightened, they plunged in, and all got** safely over but the medicine man's little son; he was drowned.

The medicine man mourned bitterly for his son, for he thought it was he that had caused the little boy's death.

Believing as he did that the world was full of spirits, every Indian hoped that one of them would come to him and be his protector, especially in war. When a lad became about seventeen years of age, his parents would say, "You are now old enough to go to war; but you should first go out and find your god!" They meant by this, that he should not risk his life in battle until he had a protecting spirit.

Finding one's god was not an easy task. The lad painted his body with white clay, as if in mourning, and went out among the hills, upon some bluff, where he could be seen of the gods; and for days, with neither food nor drink, and often torturing himself, he cried to the gods to pity him and come to him. His sufferings at last brought on delirium, so that he dreamed, or saw a vision. Whatever he saw in this vision was his god, come to pledge him protection. Usually this god was a bird or beast; or it might be the spirit of some one dead; the bird or beast was not a flesh-and-blood animal, but a spirit.

The lad then returned home. As soon as he was recovered from his fast, he set out to kill an animal like that seen in his vision, and its dried skin, or a part of it, he kept as his sacred object, or medicine, for in this sacred object dwelt his god. Thus if an otter god appeared to him, the lad would kill an otter, and into its skin, which the lad kept, the god entered. The otter skin was now the lad's medicine; he prayed to it and bore it with him to war, that his god might be present to protect him.

Indians even made offerings of food to their sacred objects. They knew the sacred object did not eat the food; but they believed that the god, or spirit, in the sacred object, ate the spirit of the food. They also burned cedar incense to their sacred objects.

The story of my uncle Wolf Chief, as he was afterwards called; will show what sufferings a young man was willing to endure who went out to seek his god. He was but seventeen when his father, Small Ankle, said to him, " My son, I think you should go out and seek your god!" The next morning my uncle climbed a high butte overlooking the Missouri, and prayed:

"O gods, I am poor; I lead a poor life;
  Make me a good man, a brave warrior!
  I want to be a great warrior;
  I want to capture many horses;
  I want to teach much to my people;
  I want to be their chief and save them in their need!"

For three days and nights, my uncle prayed; and in this time he had not a mouthful of food, not a drop of water to drink. The fourth day his father came to him. " My son," he said, " perhaps the gods would have you become a great man : and they are trying you, whether you are worthy, You have not suffered enough!"

" I am ready, father," said my uncle.

Small Ankle fixed a stout post in the ground and

fastened my uncle to it with thongs, so that all day he was in great suffering.

In the evening, Small Ankle came and cut him loose. "You have suffered enough, my son," he said; "I think the gods will now pity you and give you a dream!"

He took my uncle home and gave him something to eat and drink; then he laid the boy tenderly upon a pile of buffalo skins, before his own medicines.

For a long time, my uncle could not sleep for the pain from his wounds. A little before daylight, he fell into a troubled dream. He heard a man outside, walking around the earth lodge. The man was singing a mystery song; now and then he paused and cried, "You have done well, Strong Bull!"

Small Ankle was very happy when my uncle awoke and told him his dream. He knew that one of the gods had now come to his son to protect him and help him; and he called the boy by his new name, Strong Bull, that the god had given him.

Other men had different dreams. My grandfather once told me of a man who had a vision of four buffalo skulls that became alive.

Many years ago when our villages were on Knife River

Buffalo Skulls.

a man named Bush went out to find his god. He sought a vision from the buffalo spirits; and he thought to make himself suffer so that the spirits might pity him. He tied four buffalo skulls in a train, one behind another, and as Bush walked he dragged the train of skulls behind him.

He made his way painfully up the Missouri, mourning and crying to the gods. The banks of the Missouri are much cut up by ravines, and Bush suffered greatly as he dragged the heavy skulls over this rough country.

Fifty miles north of the villages, he came to the Little Missouri, a shallow stream, but subject to sudden freshets; he found the river flooded, and rising.

He stood on the bank and cried: " O gods, I am poor and I suffer! I want to find my god. Other men have suffered, and found their gods. Now I suffer much, but no god answers me. I am going to plunge into this torrent. I think I shall die, yet I will plunge in. O gods, if you are going to answer me, do it now and save me!"

He waded in, dragging the heavy skulls after him. The water grew deeper. He could no longer wade, he had to swim; he struck out.

He wondered that he no longer felt the weight of the skulls, and that he did not sink. The he heard something behind him cry, " *Whoo-oo-ooh!*" He looked around. The four buffalo skulls were swimming about him, buoying him up; but they were no longer skulls! Flesh and woolly hair covered them; they had big, blue eyes; they had red tongues. They were alive!

Bush himself told this story to my grandfather.

It should not be thought that Bush was trying to deceive when he said he saw these things. If one had been with him when he sprang into the torrent, and had cried, " Bush, the skulls are not alive; it is your delirium

that makes you think they live!" he would have
answered, " Of course you cannot see they are alive!
The vision is to me, not to you. The flesh and hair and
eyes are spirit flesh. I see them; you see only the
skulls!"

A man might go out many times thus, to find his
god. If he had ill success in war, or if sickness or mis-
fortune came upon him, he would think the gods had
forgotten him; and he would throw away his moccasins,
cut his hair as for mourning, paint his face with white
clay, and again cry to the gods for a vision.

A medicine man's visions were like other men's;
but we gave them more heed, because we thought he
had more power with the gods. We looked upon a
medicine man as a prophet; his dreams and visions
were messages to us from the spirits; and we thought
of his mystery power as white men think of a prophet's
power to work miracles. Our medicine men sought
visions for us, and messages from the gods, just as
white men's preachers study to tell them what God
speaks to them in His Book.

A medicine man had much influence in the tribe. He
cured our sick, called the buffalo herds to us, gave us
advice when a war party was being formed, and in
times of drought prayed for rain.

Worshipping as we did many gods, we Indians did
not think it strange that white men prayed to another
God; and when missionaries came, we did not think
it wrong that they taught us to pray to their God,
but that they said we should not pray to our own
gods. " Why," we asked, " do the missionaries hate
our gods? We do not deny the white men's Great
Spirit; why, then, should they deny our gods?"

Sometimes Indians who seek to join the mission church, secretly pray to their own gods; more often an Indian who accepts Jesus Christ and tries to follow Him, still fears his old gods, although he no longer prays to them.

Many older Indians, who do not know English, look upon Jesus Christ as they would upon one of their own gods; a story will show how His mission is sometimes misunderstood.

On this reservation lives a medicine woman, named Minnie Enemy Heart. When a girl, she went to the mission school and learned something about Jesus Christ. Afterward, as her fathers had done, she went into the hills to seek her god. She says that she fasted and prayed, and Jesus came to her in a vision. One side of his body was dark, like an Indian; the other side was white, like a white man. In His white hand he carried a lamb; in the other, a little dog.

Jesus explained the vision. " My body," He said, " half dark and half white, means that I am as much an Indian as I am a white man. This dog means that Indian ways are for Indians, as white ways are for white men; for Indians sacrifice dogs, as white men once sacrificed lambs. If the missionaries tell you this is not true, ask them who crucified me, were they Indians or white men?"

Many Indians believe this vision. More than fifteen have left the Catholic priest to follow Minnie Enemy Heart, and three or four have left our Protestant mission.

To us Indians, the spirit world seemed very near, and we did nothing without taking thought of the gods. If we would begin a journey, form a war party, hunt, trap eagles, or fish, or plant corn, we first prayed to the spirits. A bad dream would send the bravest war party hurrying home.

If our belief seem strange to white men, theirs seemed just as strange to us.

INDIAN BELIEFS

MANY medicine men added to their mystery power by owning sacred bundles, neatly bound bundles of skin or cloth, containing sacred objects or relics that had been handed down from old times. Every bundle had its history, telling how the bundle began and what gods they were that helped those who prayed before it. There were about sixty of these sacred bundles in the tribe, when I was a boy.

Medicine Post and Sacred Bundle.

The owner of a sacred bundle was called its keeper; he usually kept it hung on his medicine post, in the back part of his lodge. A sacred bundle was looked

30

upon as a kind of shrine, and in some lodges strangers were forbidden to walk between it and the fire.

When a keeper became old, he sold his sacred bundle to some younger man, that its rites might not die with him. The young man paid a hundred tanned buffalo skins and a gun or pony, and made a feast for the keeper; at this feast, the young man received the bundle with

Shrine and Sacred Bundle of the Big Birds' Ceremony.

the rites and songs that went with it. This was called, "making a ceremony."

White men think it strange that we Indians honored these sacred bundles; but I have heard that in Europe men once honored relics, the skull, or a bone, or a bit of hair of some saint, or a nail from Jesus' cross; that they did not pray to the relic, but thought that the spirit of the saint was near; or that he was more willing to hear their prayers when they knelt before the relic.

In much the same way, we Indians honored our sacred bundles. They contained sacred objects, or relics, that had belonged each to some god—his scalp, or skull, the pipe he smoked, or his robe. We did not pray to the object, but to the god or spirit to whom it had belonged, and we thought these sacred objects had wonderful power, just as white men once thought they could be cured of sickness by touching the bone of some saint.

A medicine man's influence was greater if he owned a sacred bundle. Men then came to him not only because the spirits answered him when he fasted, but because, as its keeper, he had power from the gods of the sacred bundle.

The most famous of these sacred bundles belonged to my grandfather, Small Ankle. It was called the bundle of the Big Birds' ceremony. It was kept on a kind of stand in the back part of our lodge, and it contained two skulls and a carved wooden pipe. These objects were thought to be very holy.

When my tribe came up the Missouri to Like-a-fish-hook Bend, where they built their last village, they first camped there in tepees. A question arose as to how they should plan their village, and the more important medicine men of the tribe came and sat in a circle, to consider what to do. This was seven years after the small-pox year.

At that time, the skulls of the Big Birds' ceremony were owned by an old man named Missouri River. The other medicine men, knowing that these skulls were most important sacred objects in the tribe, said to Missouri River, " Your gods are most powerful. Tell us how we should lay out our village!"

Missouri River brought the two skulls from his tent, and holding one in either hand, he walked around in a wide circle, returning again to the place where he had started. "We will leave this circle open, in the center of our village," he said. "So shall we plan it!"

He laid the skulls on the grass and said to Big Cloud, Small Ankle's son-in-law, "Your gods are powerful. Choose where you will build your earth lodge!"

Big Cloud arose. "I will build it here," he said, "where lie the two skulls. The door shall face the west, for my gods are eagles that send thunder, and eagles and thunders come from the west. And so I think we shall have rain, and our children and our fields shall thrive, and we shall live here many years." Big Cloud had once seen a vision of thunder eagles, awake and with his eyes open.

The medicine men said to Has-a-game-stick, "You choose a place for your lodge!"

Has-a-game-stick stood and said, "My god is the Sunset Woman. I want my lodge to face the sunset, that the Sunset Woman may remember me, and I will pray to her that the village may have plenty and enemies may never take it, and I think the Sunset Woman will hear me!"

The medicine men said to Bad Horn, "You stand up!"

Bad Horn stood and said, "My gods are bears, and bears always make the mouths of their dens open toward the north. I want my lodge door to open toward the north, that my bear gods may remember me. And I will pray to them that this village may stand many years!"

The medicine men then said to Missouri River, "Choose a place for your lodge!"

Missouri River took the two skulls, one in either hand, and singing a mystery song, walked around the circle with his right hand toward the center, as moves the sun. Three times he walked around, the fourth time he stopped at a place and prayed, " My gods, you are my protectors, protect also this village. Send also rains that our grain may grow, and our children may eat and be strong and healthy. So shall we prosper, because my sacred bundle is in the village."

He turned to the company upon the grass. " Go, the rest of you," he said, " and choose where you will build your lodges; and keep the circle open, as I have marked!"

Before Missouri River died, he sold his sacred bundle to my grandfather, Small Ankle; and Small Ankle sold it to his son, Wolf Chief. After Wolf Chief became a Christian, he sold the bundle to a man in New York, that it might be put into a museum.

We had other beliefs, besides these of the gods.

We thought that all little babies had lived before, most of them as birds, or beasts, or even plants. My father, Son-of-a-Star, claimed he could even remember what bird he had been.

We believed that many babies came from the babes' lodges. There were several of these. One was near our villages on the Knife River. It was a hill of yellow sand, with a rounded top like the roof of an earth lodge. In one side was a little cave, and the ground about the cave's mouth was worn smooth, as if children played there. Sometimes in the morning, little footprints were found in the sand.

To this hill a childless wife would come to pray for a son or daughter. She would lay a pair of very beautiful child's moccasins at the mouth of the cave and pray: " I am poor. I am lonesome. Come to me, one

of you! I love you. I long for you!" We understood
that children who came from this babes' lodge had
light skin and yellowish hair, like yellow sand.

A very old man once said to me: "I remember my
former life. I lived in a babes' lodge. It was like a
small earth lodge inside. There was a pit before the
door, crossed by a log. Many of the babes, trying to
cross the pit, fell in. But I walked the whole length
of the log; hence I have lived to be an old man." I
have heard this story from other old men.

Very small children, who died before they teethed
or were old enough to laugh, were not buried upon
scaffolds with our other dead, but were wrapped in skins
and placed in trees. We thought if such a baby died,
that its spirit went back to live its former life again,
as a bird, or plant, or as a babe in one of the babes'
lodges.

Older children and men and women, when they died,
went to the ghosts' village. This was a big town of
earth lodges, where the dead lived very much as they
had lived on earth. Older Indians of my tribe still
believe in the ghosts' village.

There were men in my tribe who had died, as we
believed, and gone to the ghosts' village, and come
back to life again. From these men we learned what
the ghosts' village was like.

My mother's grandfather came back thus, from the
ghosts' village; his name was *It-si-di-shi-di-it-a-ka*, or
Old Yellow Elk.

Old Yellow Elk had an otter skin for his medicine,
or sacred object. He died in the small-pox year; and his
family laid his body out on a hill with the otter skin
under his head for a pillow. Logs were piled about

the body, to keep off wolves. Men were dying so fast that there was no time to make burial scaffolds.

That night a voice was heard calling from the hill, "*A-ha-he! A-ha-he!* Come for me, I want to get up!"

The villagers ran to the grave and took away the logs, and Old Yellow Elk arose and came home.

"The ghosts' village is a fine town," he told his family. "I saw many people there, they gave me a spotted pony. My god, the otter, brought me back. He led me up the bed of the Missouri, under the water. I brought my pony with me and tied him to a log on my grave!"

His family went out to the grave the next morning and looked for the pony's tracks, but found none!

All these things I firmly believed, when I was a boy.

V

SCHOOL DAYS

I WAS six years old when Mr. Hall, a missionary, came to us, from the Santee Sioux. He could not speak the Mandan or the Hidatsa language, but he spoke Sioux, which some of our people understood. He was a good singer; and he had a song which he sang with Sioux words. Our people would crowd about him to hear it, for it was the first Christian song they had ever heard.

The song began:

> "Ho washte, ho washte,
> On Jesus yatan miye;
> Ho wakan, ho wakan,
> Nina hin yeyan!"

The words are a translation of an English hymn:

The Sun Man (Redrawn from a sketch by Goodbird).

"Sweetly sing, sweetly sing,
Jesus is our Saviour king;
Let us raise. let us raise,
High our notes of praise!"

It is a custom of my people to give a name to every stranger who comes among us, either from some singularity in his dress or appearance, or from something that he says or does. Our people caught the first two words of the missonary's song and named him after them, Ho Washte. He is still called by this name.

Mr. Hall had brought his wife with him, and they began building a house with timbers freighted up the river on a steamboat. Our chief, Crow's Belly, threatened to burn the house, but the missionary made him a feast and explained that he wanted to use the house for a school, where Indian children could learn English. Crow's Belly thought this a good plan, and made no further trouble.

The school was opened the next winter. It was soon noised in the village that English would be taught in the mission school, and several young men started to attend, my uncle, Wolf Chief, among them. They went each morning with hair newly braided, faces painted, and big brass rings on their fingers. Most of them found school work rather hard, and soon tired of it.

The next fall, my parents started me to school, for my father wanted me to learn English. The mission house was a half mile from our village; I went each morning with a little Mandan companion, named Hollis Montclair, We wore Indian dress, leggings, moccasins, and leather shirt.

At noon Hollis and I would return to the village for our noon meal; and sometimes we would go to school again in the afternoon. We went pretty faithfully all the fall, and until Christmas time, when our teacher told us we were to have a Christmas tree.

Hollis and I had never seen a Christmas tree; and when Christmas day came, we could hardly wait until the time came for us to go to the school house. It was a cheerful scene then, that met our eyes. The tree was a cedar cut on the Missouri bottoms, lighted, and trimmed with strips of bright colored paper. Mr. Hall and his family sat at the front, smiling. My teacher moved about among the children, greeting each as he arrived, and speaking a kind word to those that were shy. About fifteen school children of the age of Hollis and myself were present.

We had music and singing, and Mr. Hall explained what Christmas means, that it is the birthday of Jesus, the Son of God; and that we should be happy because He loved us. Presents were then given us; each child was called by name, and handed a little gift taken from the tree.

And now I grieve to say, that Hollis and I acted as badly as two white children. There was a magnet hanging on the tree, a piece of steel shaped like a horse shoe, that picked up bits of iron. Hollis and I thought it the most wonderful thing we had ever seen. We each hoped to receive it; but it was given to another child. This vexed us; and we left upon the floor the gifts we had received, and stalked out of the room. The last thing I saw as I went out of the door was my teacher with her handkerchief to her eyes. I did not feel happy when I thought of this; but I was an Indian boy, and I was not going to forgive her for not giving me the magnet!

I told the story of the magnet to my parents; and finding I was unwilling to go back to the mission, they sent me to the government school that our agent had just opened; but I did not go there long. I was taken sick, and my former teacher came to see me in our earth lodge. She was so kind and forgiving that I forgot all about the magnet, and when I got well I went back to the mission school.

I grew to love my teacher, although I was always a little afraid of her. We boys were not allowed to talk in study hours; but when our teacher's back was turned, we would whisper to one another. Sometimes our teacher turned quickly, and if she caught any of us whispering, she would come and give each of us a spat on the head with a book; but it did not hurt much, so we did not care.

We used to sing a good deal in the school. One song I liked was, " I need Thee every hour." I loved to sing, although the songs we learned were very different from our Indian songs. Indians are fond of music; I have known my grandfather and three or four cronies to sit at our lodge fire an entire night, drumming and singing, and telling stories.

I found English a rather hard language to learn. Many of the older Indians would laugh at any who tried to learn to read. " You want to forsake your Indian ways and be white men," they would say; but there were many in the village who wanted their children to learn English.

My grandfather was deeply interested in my studies. " It is their books that make white men strong," he would say. " The buffaloes will soon be killed; and we Indians must learn white ways, or starve." He was a progressive old man.

I am sorry to say that I played hookey sometimes. Big dances were often held in the village; especially, when a war party came in with a scalp, there was great excitement. The scalp was raised aloft on a pole, and the women danced about it, screaming, and singing glad songs. Warriors painted their faces with charcoal, and danced, sang, yelled, and boasted of their deeds. Everybody feasted and made merry.

When I knew that a dance was going to be held, I would hide somewhere in the village, instead of going to school. The next day my teacher would say, " Where were you yesterday?" "At the dance," I would answer. She would then tell me how naughty I was; but she never punished me, for she knew if she did, I would leave the school. My parents also scolded, but did not punish me. I am afraid I was a bad little boy!

One day, on my way to school, I was overtaken by a very old white man, with white hair. I had been going to school about a year and could talk a little English.

" What is your name, little fellow? " the old man asked. He had a friendly voice.

" My name is Goodbird," I answered.

" But what is your English name? "

" I have none."

" Then I will give you mine," the old man said, smiling. " It is Edward Moore."

It is a common custom for an Indian to give his name to a friend; so I did not know the old man's words were said in fun. At the school, I told Mr. Hall what the old man had said, and he laughed. " I think Moore is not a good name for you," he said. " Moore sounds like *moor*, a marshy place where mists rise in the air, but Edward is a very good name."

So I have called myself Edward Goodbird ever since.

Every Friday Mr. Hall gave a dinner in the mission house to his pupils. We Indian children thought these dinners wonderful. Many of us had never tasted white men's food; some things, as sour pickles, we did not like. Mr. Hall wanted us to learn to eat white bread and biscuits, so that we would ask our mothers to bake bread at home. He hoped this would be a means of getting us to like white men's ways.

On Saturdays we had no school, and Mr. Hall would go around the village, shaking hands with the Indians and inviting them to come to church the next morning. Later, Poor Wolf acted as his crier, and on Saturday evenings he would go around, calling out, " *Ho Washte, Ho Washte!* Come you people, to-morrow, and sit for him ! " He meant for them to come to church the next morning and sit in chairs.

Mr. Hall's janitor, a young Indian named Bear's Teeth, swept out the mission house, made the fires, and got the school room ready for the services. There was no bell on the mission, so a flag was run up as a signal for the congregation to gather.

Not many came to the services, fifteen or twenty were a usual congregation, sometimes only ten. Mr. Hall preached, and to make his sermons plainer, he often drew pictures on the blackboard.

My father thought the missionary's religion was good, but would not himself forsake the old ways. " The old gods are best for me," he used to say, but he let me go to hear Mr. Hall preach. I cannot say that I always understood the sermon. Sometimes Mr. Hall would say, " Thirty years ago, my friends, I saw the light!" I thought he meant he had seen a vision.

But I learned a good deal from Mr. Hall's preaching; and my lessons and the songs I learned at school made me think of Jesus; but I thought an Indian could be a Christian and also believe in the old ways.

It came over me one day, that this could not be. A story of our Indian god, *It-si-ka-ma-hi-di*, tells us that the sun is a man, with his body painted red, like fire; that the earth is flat, and that the sky covers it like a bowl turned bottom up; but in my geography, at school, I learned that the earth is round.

In our earth lodge, that night, I said to my parents, " This earth is round; the sun is a burning ball!" My cousin Butterfly was disgusted. " That is white man's talk," he grunted. " This earth is flat. White men are foolish!" This I would in no wise admit, and I came home almost daily with some new proof that the earth was round.

As I grew older and began to read books, I thought of myself as a Christian, but more because I went to the mission school, than because I thought of Jesus as my Saviour. I loved to read the stories of the Bible; and Mr. Hall taught me the Ten Commandments. Some of the Indian boys learned to swear, from hearing white men; but I never did, because Mr. Hall told me it was wrong. I thought that those who did as the Bible bade, would grow up to be good men.

I had a cousin, three years older than myself, in the Santee Indian school, who had become a Christian.

One day I received a letter from him. "I believe in Jesus' way," he wrote. " I believe Jesus is a good Saviour. I have tried His way, and I want you to try to join in and have Him for your Saviour." This letter set me to thinking.

In these years, my life outside the school room was wholly Indian. We Hidatsa children knew nothing of base ball, or one hole cat, or other white children's games, but we had many Indian games that we played. Some of these games I think better than those now played on our reservation.

In March and early April, we boys played the hoop game. A level place, bare of snow, was found, and the boys divided into two sides, about thirty yards apart. Small hoops, covered with a lacing of thongs, were rolled forward, and were caught by those of the opposite side on sticks, thrust or darted through the lacings. A hoop so

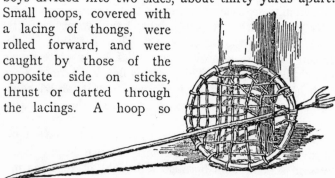

Hoop and Stick of the Hoop Game.

caught, was sent hurtling through the air, the object being to hit some one of the opposing players.

The game was played but a few weeks, for as soon as the ice broke on the Missouri, we boys went to the high bank of the river, and hurled our hoops into the current. We were told, and really believed, that they became dead buffaloes as soon as they had passed out of sight, beyond the next point of land. Such buffaloes, drowned in the thin ice of autumn and frozen in, came floating down the river in large numbers at the spring break-up. The carcasses were always fat, and the frozen flesh was sweet and tender.

After the first thunder in spring, we played *u-a-ki-he-ke*, or throw stick. Willow rods were cut, peeled, and dried, and then stained red, with ochre, or a bright green, with grass. These rods, darted against the ground, rebounded to a great distance. The player won whose rod went farthest. *U-a-ki-he-ke* is still played on the reservation.

War Bonnet
(On Lodge Post).

In June, when the rising waters have softened the river's clay banks, we fought sham battles. Each boy cut a willow withe, as long as a buggy whip, and on the smaller end squeezed a lump of wet clay. With the withe as a sling, he could throw the clay ball to an astonishing distance. Hidatsa and Mandan boys often fought against one another, using these clay balls as missiles.

It was exciting play, for we fought like armies, each side trying to force the other's position; when an attack was made, a storm of mud balls would come whizzing through the air like bullets. A hit on the bare flesh stung like a real wound. Once one of my playmates was hit in the eye, and badly hurt. I was just over fourteen, when my parents let me join in the grass dance, or war dance, as the whites call it. The other dancers made me an officer, and my father was so pleased, that he hung up a fine eagle's feather war bonnet in our lodge. " If enemies come against us," he said, " my son shall go out to fight wearing this war bonnet!"

One evening, Bear's Arm, a lad of eighteen years, came in from hunting a strayed pony; he was much excited. "I saw two Sioux in war dress, hiding in a coulee," he told us.

Our warriors ran for their ponies. " Put on your war bonnet," my father said to me. " I am going to take you in the party. Keep close to me; and if there is a fight, see if you cannot strike an enemy!"

We rode all night, Bear's Arm leading us. We reached the coulee and surrounded it a little before daybreak, and with the first streak of dawn, we closed in, our rifles ready; but we found no enemies.

This was my one war exploit.

Buffaloes.

VI

HUNTING BUFFALOES

THE summer I was twelve years old, our village went on a buffalo hunt, for scouts had brought in word that herds had been sighted a hundred miles west of the Missouri. My father, Son-of-a-Star, was chosen leader of the hunt.

My tribe no longer used travois, for the government had issued wagons to us. These we took apart, loading the wheels into bull boats while the beds were floated over the river. We made our first camp at the edge of the foot hills, on the other side of the river.

The next morning, we struck tents, loaded them into our wagons, and began the march.

47

My father led, carrying his medicine bundle at his saddle head; behind him rode two or three elder Indians, leaders of the tribe, also on horseback. Then followed the wagons in a long line; and on either side rode the young men, on their tough, scrubby, little ponies.

Some of our young men as they rode, drove small companies of horses. Neighbors commonly put their horses together, and a young man, or two or three young men, acted as herders. Sometimes a girl, mounted astraddle like a man, drove them.

Now and then a youth might be seen reining in his pony to let the line of wagons pass, while he kept a sharp watch for his sweetheart. She hardly glanced at him as she rode by, for it was not proper for a young man's sweetheart to let him talk to her in the marching line. The time for courtship was in camp, in the evening.

Clay Pot with Thong Handle.

Toward five or six in the afternoon, we made camp. The wagons were drawn up in a big circle, and the women pitched the tents, while the men unhitched and hobbled their horses, and brought firewood. The women brought water and lighted the fires.

Water was carried in pails. I have heard that in old times, they used clay pots made of a kind of red clay, and burned; a thong went around the neck of the pot, for a handle.

My mother, an active woman, often had her fire started before her neighbors. While she got supper, my father sat and smoked. Friends frequently joined him, and they would sit in a circle, passing the pipe around, telling funny stories and laughing. My father was a capital story teller.

For supper we had deer or antelope meat, boiled or roasted, and my mother often fried wheat-flour dough into a kind of biscuits that were rather hard. Corn picked green the year before, and boiled and dried, was stewed in a kettle, making a dish much like the canned corn we buy at the store. More often we had succotash, hominy boiled with fat and beans. We drank black coffee, sweetened; my mother put the coffee beans into a skin, pounded them fine with an ax, and boiled them in an iron pot. You see, we were getting civilized.

When supper was ready, my mother would call " *Mi-ha-dits*—I have done!" and my father would put up his pipe and come to eat. My mother gave him meat, steaming hot, in a tin dish, and poured coffee into a cup; another cup held meat broth, which made a good drink also. We did not bring wooden feast bowls with us, as some families did.

My mother and I ate with my father, much as white families do; a robe or blanket was spread for each to sit upon.

I wore moccasins and leggings; and my hair was braided, Indian fashion, in two tails over my shoulders, but my mother had made me a white man's vest, of black cloth, embroidered all over with elk teeth. I was proud of this vest, and cared not a whit that I had no coat to wear over it.

The seventh day out, we made camp near the Cannon Ball River. My father had sent two mounted scouts ahead, with a spy glass, to see if they could find the herds; at evening, they returned with the report, " There is a big herd yonder!" Everybody got ready for the hunt the next morning, and my father made me happy by telling me that I might go along.

We arose early. My father saddled two ponies, one of them a pack animal; and I mounted a third, with a white man's saddle. My father's were pack saddles, of elk horn, covered with raw hide; ropes, looped up like a figure 8, were tied behind them to be used in binding the packs of meat we would bring home from the hunt.

There were about forty hunters in our party, mounted, and leading each a pack horse; eight boys, of twelve or fifteen years of age, and three old men. I remember one of the old men carried a bow and arrows, probably from old custom. Only the hunters expected to take part in the actual chase of the buffaloes; they were armed with rifles.

Quirt (Indian Whip.)

The party's leader, *E-di-a-ka-ta*—the same who led our tribe to the Yellowstone—rode ahead, and we followed at a brisk trot. Five miles out of camp, the two scouts were again sent ahead with the spy glass. We saw them coming back at a gallop and knew that the herd was found, and we urged our horses at the top of their speed. I remember the *slap* of the quirts on the little ponies' flanks; and the *beat-beat, beat-beat!* of their hoofs on the hard ground. Indians do not shoe their horses.

We drew rein behind a hill, a half mile to leeward of the herd, and, having dismounted, hobbled our led horses. Our hunters laid aside their shirts and leggings, stripped the saddles from their ponies' backs, and twisted bridles of thong into their ponies' mouths; it was our tribe's custom to ride bare-back in the hunt.

E-di-a-ka-ta went a little way off and stood, facing in the direction of the herd; from a piece of red cloth he tore a long strip, ripped this again into three or four pieces and laid them on the ground. I saw his lips move, and knew he was praying, but I could not hear his words. The pieces of red cloth were an offering to the spirits of the buffaloes.

Our hunters remounted and drew up in a line facing the herd, *E-di-a-ka-ta* on the right, and at a signal, the line started forward, neck-and-neck, at a brisk gallop. A guard, named *Tsa-wa*, or Bear's Chief, rode in advance; if a hunter pressed too far forward in the line, *Tsa-wa* struck the hunter's pony in the face with his quirt.

We boys and the three old men rode a little behind the line of hunters; we did not expect to take part in the hunt, but wanted to see the kill.

As we cleared the brow of the hill we sighted the buffaloes, about four hundred yards away, and *E-di-a-ka-ta* gave the signal, " *Ku'kats*—Now then!" Down came the quirts on the little ponies' flanks, making them leap forward like big cats. The line broke at once, each hunter striving to reach the herd first and kill the fattest. An iron-gray horse, I remember, was in the lead.

We boys followed at breakneck speed—unwillingly on my part; my pony had taken the bit in his mouth and was going over the stony ground at a speed that I feared would throw him any moment and break his neck and mine. I tugged at the reins and clung to the saddle, too scared to cry out.

Bang! A fat cow tumbled over. *Bang! Bang! Bang! Bang!* The frightened herd started to flee, swerved to the right, and went thundering away up wind, in a whirl of dust. Buffaloes, when alarmed, fly up wind if the way is open; their sight is poor, but they have a keen scent, and running up wind they can nose an Indian a half mile away.

For such heavy beasts, buffaloes have amazing speed, and only our fastest horses were used in hunting them; indeed, a young bull often outran our fastest ponies.

Only cows were killed. The flesh of bulls is tough and was not often eaten; that of calves crumbled when dried, making it unfit for storing.

Some buffalo calves, forsaken by the herd, were running wildly over the prairie, bleating for their mothers; two of our hunters caught one of the smallest with a lariat, and brought it to me. " Here, boy," they said, " keep this calf."

I caught the rope and drew the calf after me; but my pony, growing frightened, reared and kicked the little animal; paying out more rope, I led the calf at a safer distance from my horse's heels.

The hunters came straggling back, and my father seeing the calf, cried out, " Let that calf go! Buffaloes are sacred animals. You should not try to keep one captive!" I was much disappointed, for I wanted to take it into camp.

My father had killed three fat cows, and these he

now sought out and dressed. The shoulders, hams, and choicer cuts he loaded on our led horse, covering the pack with a green hide and tying it down with the raw-hide ropes brought for the purpose; the rest he left in a pile on the prairie, covered with the other two hides. We intended to return for these with wagons, the next day.

As my father was cutting up one of the carcasses, I saw him throw away what I thought were good

Drying Meat and Boiling Bones.

cuts; I did not like to see good meat wasted, and when I thought he was not looking, I slyly put the pieces back on the pile.

We returned to camp slowly, at times urging our ponies to a gentle trot, more often letting them walk. My father had to dismount several times to secure our pack of meat, which threatened to slip from our pack horse's back. In our tent that evening, I heard him telling my mother of my part in the hunt. " Our son," he said, " is no wasteful lad. He put back some tough leg pieces that I had thrown away. He would not see good meat wasted!" And they both laughed.

Stages were built in the camp, and for two days, every body was busy drying meat or boiling bones for marrow fat. The dried meat was packed in skin bags, or made into bundles; the marrow fat was run into bladders; and all was taken to Like-a-fish-hook village, to be stored for winter.

Goodbird at the age of twenty. (Redrawn from portrait by Julian
Scott. Report Indian Census, 1890.)

VII

FARMING

THE time came when we had to forsake our village
at Like-a-fish-hook Bend, for the government
wanted the Indians to become farmers. "You
should take allotments," our agent would say. "The
big game is being killed off, and you must plant bigger
fields or starve. The government will give you plows
and cattle."

All knew that the agent's words were true, and little
by little our village was broken up. In the summer
of my sixteenth year nearly a third of my tribe left to
take up allotments.

We had plenty of land; our reservation was twice the
size of Rhode Island, and our united tribes, with the
Rees who joined us, were less than thirteen hundred

55

souls. Most of the Indians chose allotments along the Missouri, where the soil was good and drinking water easy to get. Unallotted lands were to be sold and the money given to the three tribes.

Forty miles above our village, the Missouri makes a wide bend around a point called Independence Hill, and here my father and several of his relatives chose their allotments. The bend enclosed a wide strip of meadow land, offering hay for our horses. The soil along the river was rich and in the bottom stood a thick growth of timber.

My father left the village, with my mother and me, in June. He had a wagon, given him by the agent; this he unbolted and took over the river piece by piece, in a bull boat; our horses swam.

We camped at Independence in a tepee, while we busied ourselves building a cabin. My father cut the logs; they were notched at the ends, to lock into one another at the corners. A heavier log, a foot in thickness, made the ridge pole. The roof was of willows and grass, covered with sods.

Cracks between the logs were plastered with clay, mixed with short grass. The floor was of earth, but we had a stove.

We were a month putting up our cabin.

Though my father's coming to Independence was a step toward civilization, it had one ill effect: it removed me from the good influences of the mission school, so that for a time I fell back into Indian ways. Winter, also, was not far off; the season was too late for us to plant corn, and the rations issued to us every two weeks rarely lasted more than two or three days. To keep our family in meat, I turned hunter.

There were no buffaloes on the reservation, but black-tailed deer were plentiful, and in the hills were a good many antelopes. I had a Winchester rifle, a 40.60 caliber, and I was a good shot.

To hunt deer, I arose before daylight and went to the woods along the Missouri. Deer feed much at night, and as evening came on, they would leave the thick underbrush by the river and go into the hills to browse on the rich prairie grasses. I would creep along the edge of the woods, rifle in hand, ready to shoot any that I saw coming in from the feeding grounds.

I was careful to keep on the leeward side of the game; a deer running up wind will scent an Indian as quickly as a buffalo.

I loved to hunt, and although a mere boy, I was one of the quickest shots in my tribe. I remember that one morning I was coming around a clump of bushes when I saw a doe and buck ahead, just entering the thicket. I fired, hardly glancing at the sights; I saw the buck fall, but when I ran up I found the doe lying beside him, killed by the same bullet.

Independence was a wild spot. The hill from which the place took its name had been a favorite fasting place for young men who sought visions; at its foot, under a steep bank, swept the Missouri, full of dangerous whirlpools. Such spots, lonely and wild, we Indians thought were haunts of the spirits.

Once, when I was a small boy, my father took me to see the Sun dance. A man named Turtle-no-head was suspended from a post in a booth, and dancing around it. Turtle-no-head's hands were behind him, and he strained at the rope as he danced. Women were crying, " *A-la-la-la-la-la!* " Old men were calling out, " Good; Turtle-no-head is a man. One should be willing to suffer to find his god; then he will strike many enemies and win honors!'"

I was much stirred by what I saw, and by the old men's words.

" Father," I said, " when I get big, I am going to suffer and seek a vision, like Turtle-no-head! "

" Good! " said my father, laughing.

At Independence, I thought of this vow made years before. One day, I said to my father, " I want you to suspend me from the high bank, over the Missouri."

When evening came, my father stripped me to my clout and moccasins, and helped me paint my body with white clay. He called a man named Crow, and they took me to the bank, over the Missouri. My father fastened me to the rope, and I swung myself over the bank, hanging with my weight upon the rope. " Suffer as long as you can! " called my father, and left me.

I did not feel much pain, but I became greatly wearied from the strain upon my back and thighs. Toward morning I could stand it no longer. I drew myself up on the bank, and went home and to bed; and I slept so soundly that no dream came from the spirits.

A year later, I again sought a vision. This time my father took me to a high hill, a mile or two from the river. He drove a post into the ground, fastened me to it, as before, and left me, just at nightfall.

I threw myself back upon the rope and danced around the post, hoping to fall into a swoon and see a vision.

It was autumn, and a light snow was falling; the cold flakes on my bare shoulders made me shiver till my teeth chattered. The night was black as pitch. A coyote howled. I was so lonely that I wished a ghost would sit on the post and talk with me, though I was dreadfully afraid of ghosts, especially at night. I grew so cold that my knees knocked together.

About two o'clock in the morning, I untied the rope and went home. For an hour I felt sick, but I soon fell into a sleep, again dreamless.

I was eating my breakfast when my father came in. "I have seen no vision, father," I told him; he said nothing.

The next year the government forbade the Indians to torture themselves when they fasted. My father was quite vexed. "The government does wrong to forbid us to suffer for our gods!" he said. But I was rather glad. "The Indian's way is hard," I thought. "The white man's road is easier!" And I thought again of the mission school.

Other things drew my thoughts to civilized ways. Our agent issued to every Indian family having an allotment, a plow, and wheat, flax, and oats, for seeding. My father and I broke land near our cabin, and in the spring seeded it down.

We had a fair harvest in the fall. Threshing was done on the agency machine, and, having sacked our grain, my father and I hauled it, in four trips, to Hebron, eighty miles away. Our flax we sold for seventy-five cents, our wheat for sixty cents, and our oats for twenty-five cents a bushel. Our four loads brought us about eighty dollars.

I became greatly interested in farming. There was good soil on our allotment along the river, although our fields sometimes suffered from drought; away from the river, much of our land was stony, fit only for grazing.

My parents had been at Independence eight years, when one day the agent sent for me. I went to his office.

"I hear you have become a good farmer," he said, as I came in. "I want to appoint you assistant to our agency farmer. Your district will include all allotments west of the Missouri between the little Missouri and Independence. I will pay you three hundred dollars a year. Will you accept?"

"I will try what I can do," I answered.

"Good," said the Major. "Now for your orders! You are to measure off for every able-bodied Indian, ten acres of ground to be plowed and seeded. If an Indian is lazy and will not attend to his plowing, report him to me and I will send a policeman. In the fall, you are to see that every family puts up two tons of hay for each horse or steer owned by it."

I did not know what an acre was. "It is a piece of ground," the agent explained, "ten rods wide and sixteen rods long." From this I was able to compute pretty well how much ten acres should be; but I am not sure that all the plots I measured were of the same size.

I began my new duties at once, and at every cabin in my district, I measured off a ten-acre plot and explained the agent's orders. Not a few of the Indians had done some plowing at Like-a-fish-hook village, and all were willing to learn. Once a month, I took a blacksmith around to inspect the Indians' plows.

Rains were abundant that summer, and the Indians had a good crop. Some families harvested a hundred bushels of wheat from a ten-acre field; others, seventy-five bushels; and some had also planted oats.

The government began to issue cattle in payment of lands sold for us. The first issue was one cow to each family, and the agent ordered me to see that every family built a barn.

These barns were put up without planks or nails. A description of my own will show what they were like; it rested on a frame of four forked posts, with stringers laid in the forks; puncheons, or split logs, were leaned against the stringers for walls; rough-cut rafters supported a roofing of willows and dry grass, earthed over with sods.

More cattle were issued to us until we had a considerable herd at Independence. The cattle were let run at large, but each steer or cow was branded by its owner. Calves ran with their mothers until fall; the herd was then corralled and each calf was branded with its mother's brand. My own brand was the letters SU on the right shoulder.

Herders guarded our cattle during the calving season; we paid them ten cents for every head of stock herded through the summer months.

I had been assistant farmer six years and our herd had grown to about four hundred head, when Bird Bear and Skunk, our two herders, reported that some of our cattle had strayed. "We have searched the coulees and thickets, but cannot find them," they said. Branding time came; we corralled the herd and found about fifty head missing.

We now suspected that our cattle had been stolen. Cattle thieves, we knew, were in the country; they had broken into a corral one night, on a ranch not far from Independence and killed a cowboy named Long John.

Winter had passed, when the agent called me one day

into his office. "Goodbird," he said, "I want you to take out a party of our agency police and find those thieves who stole your cattle. Start at once!"

I got my party together, eight in all; Hollis Montclair, my boyhood chum; Frank White Calf, Crow Bull, Sam Jones, White Owl, Little Wolf, No Bear, and myself. Only Hollis and I spoke English.

We started toward the Little Missouri, where we suspected the thieves might be found. I drove a wagon with our provisions and tent; my men were mounted. We reached the Little Missouri before nightfall, and camped.

The next morning, we turned westward; before noon, we crossed a prairie dog village, and shot three or four prairie dogs for dinner. The hair was singed off the carcasses, and they were drawn, and spitted on sticks over the fire. Prairie dogs are not bad eating, especially in the open air, by a good wood fire; I have never become so civilized that I would not rather eat out of doors.

Prairie Dogs.

Toward evening we met a cowboy. "How!" I called, as I drew in my team. "Have you seen any stray cattle, with Indian brands, ID, 7 bar, 7, or the like?" And I told him of our missing cattle.

"I know where they are," said the cowboy. "You will find them on a ranch near Stroud's post-office; but don't tell who told you!"

"Have no fear," I answered.

Stroud's post-office was farther west, near the Montana border; we reached it the third or fourth day out.

We made camp, and after supper, I went in and told Mr. Stroud our errand.

"Yes," he said, "your cattle are three miles from here, on a ranch owned by Frank Powers; he hired two cowboys to steal them for him."

The next morning my men and I mounted, and leaving our wagon at Stroud's, started for Powers' ranch. I was unarmed; the others of my party had their rifles.

We stopped at the cabin of a man named Crockin, to inquire our way. A white man came in; after he had gone out again, I asked Crockin, "Who is that man?"

"He is Frank Powers," said Crockin.

I turned to my men and said in their own language, "That is the man who stole our cattle."

Little Wolf drew his cleaning rod. "I am going to give that bad white man a beating," he cried angrily.

"You will not," I answered. "We will go into Powers' pasture and round up his cattle; and I will cut out all that I think are ours. If that bad white man comes out and says evil words against me, do nothing. If he shoots at me, kill him quick; but do not you shoot first!"

My men loaded their rifles, and about two o'clock I led them into the pasture. Powers' cattle were all bunched in a big herd; we drove them to a grassy flat, and I began cutting out those that were ours.

Powers saw us and came out, revolver in hand, and two or three white men joined him. He was so angry that he acted like a mad man; he grew red in the face, talked loud, and swore big oaths; but he did not shoot, for he knew my men would kill him.

I cut about twenty-five head out of the herd, all that I found with altered brands on the right shoulder or thigh. Maybe I took some of Powers' cattle by mistake, but I did not care much.

Powers left us after a while. My men rounded up our cattle, and we drove them back to Stroud's and camped.

After supper, I asked Mr. Stroud to write a letter to our agent, telling him what I had done. "To-morrow," I told my men, "we will set out for home. You drive our cattle back to the reservation in short stages, so that they will not sicken with the heat. I will go ahead with Mr. Stroud's letter."

I set out before sunrise; at four o'clock I reached Independence, eighty miles away; and at sunset, I was at Elbowoods.

It was Decoration day, and the Indians were having a dance. The agent was sitting in his office with the inspector, from Washington.

"I have found our cattle," I said; and I gave him Mr. Stroud's letter.

He read it and handed it to the inspector.

"Report this matter to the United States marshal," the inspector said to him. "Tell him to have Powers arrested."

The Chapel at Independence.

VIII

THE WHITE MAN'S WAY

MY thirty-fifth winter—as we Indians count years—found me still assistant farmer; but time had brought many changes to our reservation. Antelope and blacktailed deer had gone the way of the buffalo. A few earth lodges yet stood, dwellings of stern old warriors who lived in the past; but the Indian police saw that every child was in school learning the white man's way. A good dinner at the noon hour made most of the children rather willing scholars.

The white man's peace had stopped our wars with the Sioux; and the young folks of either tribe visited, and made presents to one another. I had visited the Standing Rock Sioux, and had learned to rather like them. Indeed, I liked one Sioux girl so well that I married her. We had a comfortable cabin; my wife was a good cook, and my children were in school.

Living so far from the mission, it was not possible for me to attend church services at the mission house; but Mr. Hall came to Independence and preached to us. Until a school house was built, he often held his meetings in my cabin.

I usually interpreted for him. He would speak in English and I would translate into Hidatsa, which the Mandans also understand. Indians are good linguists; not a few young men of my tribe speak as many as four or five languages.

I drew no salary as interpreter; but I felt myself well repaid by what I learned of the Bible. Interpreting Mr. Hall's sermons made them sink into my heart, so that I would think of them as I went about my work.

As time went on, there grew up quite a company of Christians at Independence. One of their active leaders was Frank White Calf; and he and Sitting Crow called a kind of praying council at Two Chiefs' cabin. All the Independence Christians came; and I was invited to meet them.

Some of the Indians prayed; and Frank White Calf asked me, " Goodbird, why do you not join us in this Christian way? Tell us your mind!"

I arose and spoke: " My friends, I learned of this Christian way at the mission school. It is a good way. You ask me my thoughts. I answer, I have tried to live like a Christian and I love to read my Bible, but I have not received baptism; I am now ready to be baptized."

A few days after this, Frank White Calf said to me,

"Mr. Hall wants you to come to the mission house and be baptized."

I went the next Sunday with my family, and was received into the church. My sons Charles and Alfred were baptized at the same time.

In part, I was influenced to become a church member by the thought that it was the white man's way. Our Indian beliefs, I felt sure, were doomed; for white men's customs were becoming stronger with us each year. " I am traveling the new way, now!" I thought, when I was baptized. " I can never go back to Indian ways again."

But for some years, even after I became a church member, I was not a very firm Christian; and I did not keep God's commandments very well, because I did not believe all that the missionaries taught me. I was unwilling to trust any white man's words, until I had proved that they were true. I did not want to take anything on faith.

Mr. Hall made Independence a preaching station, and put an assistant in charge; I interpreted for her. Sometimes Mr. Hall, or his son, preached to us.

The missionary teacher let me know each week what was to be the next Sunday's lesson, and she gave me books to read. Knowing something of her subject, I was better able to interpret for her. In this way, also, I learned more of Christ's teachings; and I learned how to study my Bible.

This study of the Bible influenced me a great deal; and my having to interpret made me fall into the habit of going to church regularly. My interest in church work grew.

In 1903, the government abolished the position of

assistant farmer. In October of the following year, Mr. Hall's son said to me, "We need an assistant missionary at Independence, and my father and I want to appoint you. Come and talk with my father about it."

I went to Elbowoods and saw Mr. Hall. "Edward," he asked, "are you willing to be our assistant missionary?"

"Yes," I answered.

I knew some one must preach to the Independence Indians; and I thought I could do this, because I could speak their language as well as read English. I felt also that I was closer to God than I had been when I was baptized.

So I became Mr. Hall's assistant, and have been in charge of the Independence station ever since. Every Sunday I preach to the Indians in the Hidatsa language. My text is the Sunday-school lesson of the week, for we Indians do not care for sermons, such as white men hear. Our older men cannot read English, and we do not have the Bible in our own tongue; we like best to hear the Sunday-school lesson because it explains the stories of the Bible, which my people cannot read for themselves.

Things do not always go smoothly in an Indian congregation. Frictions and misunderstandings arise, as I have heard they do in white churches; and Indians sometimes seek to become church members from unworthy motives. Our former life makes us Indians clannish; members of the same clan feel bound to help one another, and many Indians seem to look upon the church as a kind of clan. Sometimes a young man will say, "I will be baptized and join your church. Then all the Christians will work to make me agency police-man!"

Others, again, will say, " I want to join the church because I am sick; perhaps God will make me well!"

Some, with clearer faith, say, " I want to become a Christian because I believe Jesus will save me to be a spirit with Him." They mean that they hope Jesus will take them to live with Him when they die.

My uncle, Wolf Chief, says of the Christian way: " I traveled faithfully the way of the Indian gods, but they never helped me. When I was sick, I prayed to them, but they did not make me well. I prayed to them when my children died; but they did not answer me. I have but two children left, and I am going to trust God to keep these that they do not die like the others. I talk to God every day, as I would talk to my father; and I ask Him for everything I want. I try to do all that He bids me do. I hope that He will take my spirit to travel in that new heaven about which I have learned. I cannot change now. I can never go back to the old gods!"

Wolf Chief has been a strong Christian for more than eight years. He has given much to our mission work; and he is never absent from Sunday services.

Six years ago, we Christians at Independence became dissatisfied with our log meeting house, and began to talk of building a chapel, or church-house, as we call it. A council was called in Wolf Chief's cabin.

It was an evening in December; all the leading Christians of Independence came with their wives— Wolf Chief, Tom Smith, Frank White Calf, Mike Basset, Hollis Montclair, Sam Jones, Louis Baker, and myself. Each woman brought something for a feast, and we ate together. We had fried bread, tea, pie, tomato soup, and other good things.

When our feasting was over, Wolf Chief made a speech. " We Christian Indians," he said, " should have a chapel. We should raise the money to build a house to God, where we can go and worship!"

Tom Smith and others spoke, and we called for subscriptions. Frank White Calf's wife gave five dollars. Wolf Chief's brother, Charging Enemy, although not a Christian, gave a pony. Others promised, some ten, some fifteen, and some twenty-five dollars.

I was appointed treasurer to make collections, and get more subscriptions. I wrote a letter to Water Chief's dancing society and asked them to give something. The dancing Indians are pagans; but they gave us a subscription.

Mr. Hall gave us fifty dollars; Mr. Shultis, our school-teacher, gave us ten dollars; and other white friends gave us subscriptions; but most of the money was given by the Indians.

When we had collected three hundred and fifty dollars, we began buying lumber.

Wolf Chief wanted to give us the land for our chapel; but the Indian commissioner wrote, " No, you may sell your land, but you must not give it away." So we bought the land for a dollar an acre; but Wolf Chief gave the money back to us, outwitting the commissioner after all!

We bought ten acres. " When white men build a house," said Wolf Chief, " they leave land around it for a yard. We should be ashamed not to have some land around God's house!" Our ten-acre plot makes a fine big church yard; at one end is our Indian cemetery.

Wolf Chief also gave us a colt, and much money, and bought paint and nails.

We Indians think Wolf Chief wealthy. He owns five hundred acres of land, thirty head of cattle, eight horses, and pigs and chickens; he has a potato field and a corn field, and owns a trading store.

More than fifty were present when we dedicated our chapel. A minister from Minneapolis preached the sermon, and I interpreted for him. A young white lady sang, and played the organ, and my cousin played a clarionet. Our school teacher had lent us his phonograph, and it sang " There are ninety and nine," just like a choir in a city church. I asked for subscriptions to clear off our debt, and we raised eighty-three dollars in money, and Wolf Chief gave us another colt. The minister prayed God to bless our chapel, and we went home, all very happy.

Older Indians, who came from Like-a-fish-hook village, find their life on allotments rather lonesome. Cabins are often two or three miles apart and the old men cannot amuse themselves with books, for they cannot read. In old times, Indians often met in big dances; but pagan ceremonies are used in these dances, and Mr. Hall does not like the Christian Indians to go to them.

That our Christian Indians may meet socially now and then, we now observe many white men's holidays; and at such times, we make our chapel the meeting place. In August, we hold a Young Men's Christian Convention, when families come from miles around, to camp in tents around the chapel. At Christmas, we have feasting and giving of presents; and our chapel is so crowded that many have to stand without, and look through the windows. Of late years, we have also observed Decoration Day at Independence.

Our camp last Decoration Day was ten or more tents, with two or three families in a tent. We made a booth, after old custom, of leafy branches and small trees. In this we gathered at about ten o'clock.

Our school teacher began our exercises with a speech telling us what Decoration Day should mean to us. We sang " America," and other hymns, and had speeches by Indians. A committee had been appointed to choose the speakers.

Rabbit Head spoke, " I do not know anything about your way, but I encourage you! Go on, do more. I have nothing against your going the Christian way! " Rabbit Head is a chief in the Grass dance society, and a pagan.

Wounded Face spoke, " I do not belong to this church, I am a Catholic; but I thus show that I like white men's ways! "

After dinner we made ready to decorate our graves. Every family having a son buried in our graveyard, hired a clan father to clean the grave of weeds and stones; if a daughter, a clan aunt was asked. An Indian calls the members of his mother's clan, his brothers and sisters; members of his father's clan, he calls his clan fathers and aunts.

At two o'clock we formed a procession and marched to the cemetery. Two aged scouts led, High Eagle and Black Chest ; High Eagle bore a large American flag. We marched by two's in a long line, the men first, then the women and children. Having marched around the graveyard, we stood and sang some hymns, and I made a speech:

" All you relatives and friends of these dead, I want to make a speech to you!

" It seems sad to our hearts to come here, and yet we are glad, because we come to remember our loved ones at their graves; so both gladness and sorrow are in our hearts.

" These warrior men, that you see here, fought against our enemies. They fought to save us, so that to-day we are not captive, but free. Some of the brave men who fought to save us, died in battle. Also, some of your loved ones have died and are buried in this grave-yard. Many of these loved ones did not die fighting against enemies, yet they were brave warriors against evil and temptation. Now they are gone from us. They are in a new world, the ghost land; they are with God. I am sure they are in a safe, happy place.

" Now come forward, all who want to put flowers on the graves."

We had had a cold, dry spring, and the prairie flowers had not come into bloom, but we had sent to Plaza and bought artificial silk flowers. The clan fathers and aunts placed these flowers on the graves, while many of the women wept.

We Hidatsas know that our Indian ways will soon perish; but we feel no anger. The government has given us a good reservation, and we think the new way better for our children.

I think God made all peoples to help one another. We Indians have helped you white people. All over this country are corn fields; we Indians gave you the seeds for your corn, and we gave you squashes and beans.   On the lakes in your parks are canoes; Indians taught you to make those canoes.

We Indians think you are but paying us back, when you give us schools and books, and teach us the new way.

For myself, my family and I own four thousand acres of land; and we have money coming to us from the government.   I own cattle and horses.   I can read English, and my children are in school.

I have good friends among the white people, Mr. Hall and others, and best of all, I think each year I know God a little better.

I am not afraid.

INDEX